THE TYLER TWINS:
MYSTERY OF THE MISSING GRANDFATHER

The Tyler Twins

MYSTERY OF THE MISSING GRANDFATHER

Hilda Stahl

WindRider BOOKS
Tyndale House Publishers, Inc., Wheaton, Illinois

First printing, December 1988

Library of Congress Catalog Card Number 88-50699
ISBN 0-8423-7630-5
Copyright 1988 by Hilda Stahl
Printed in the United States of America

*Dedicated with a heart full of love
to all the special people of the
New Life Drama Company.*

CONTENTS

ONE
Trapped!

Pam Tyler dropped her three music books on the piano bench with a loud bang. "I don't want to practice with Ellie Pepper here," she said out loud. Flushing, Pam looked back quickly at the open door of the practice room. She didn't want Mrs. James to hear and feel badly. During the summer months that Pam was living with her dad, Mrs. James was working hard to teach Pam all she could about piano. Mrs. James was nice, and she thought everyone else was, too. She didn't know that Ellie Pepper sometimes pinched Pam or sometimes wrote notes full of bad words to Pam.

Ellie wasn't supposed to be at the music center today. But just as Pam had stepped out of the room where she took her piano lessons twice a week, she saw Ellie walking down the hall.

"Hi, Pam," Ellie Pepper said, sailing into the room as if she belonged there. She wore bright flowered shorts and a red T-shirt, and she was carrying her piano practice books. Her black eyes were large in her dark-skinned face. Her teeth flashed a bright white as she smiled.

Pam hesitated, then said, "Hi, Ellie." Pam didn't want trouble, but she wasn't going to let Ellie Pepper stay. "This is my room," Pam said, "and I want to be here alone now. I'm signed up to practice for this half hour after my lesson."

Ellie wrinkled her nose and flipped her dark head back. "So what?" she asked.

Pam swallowed hard. The palms of her hands were damp with perspiration. "I don't want you in here while I'm playing," she told Ellie.

Ellie stepped right up close to Pam, which made Pam nervous since Ellie was about a half head taller than she and a year older. "I want to practice now," Ellie said in a mean voice, "and there's not room for both of us. So I guess you'll have to leave."

A shiver ran down Pam's spine. "If Terryl were here, she'd make *you* leave."

Ellie shot a look at the door, as though she was making sure Terryl wasn't there. Then she looked at Pam again. "Your twin sister doesn't scare me," she said firmly.

With a trembling hand, Pam pushed her long honey-brown hair over her slender shoulder. She should've told Terryl to stay with her instead of letting her go back to the apartment to practice her violin. Terryl didn't let anyone or anything frighten her. "Mrs. James said I could practice now, Ellie," Pam said.

Ellie marched to the piano. "Well, she's gone already, so she can't help you now."

"Why are you so mean to me?" Pam cried as she ran around Ellie and stood near the bench so

Ellie couldn't sit down. "I never did anything to hurt you."

Ellie gripped her practice books closer to her chest, "I was Mrs. James's favorite student until you came along! Now all she talks about is you!"

"That's not my fault," Pam protested.

"And you don't even have the talent that I have," Ellie went on. "My mother said so."

Pam locked her hands together behind her back. "I'm just new at piano, and Mrs. James knows I'll only be here until September first."

Ellie's face brightened. "September first? Where will you go then?"

Pam hesitated. "To live with my mom at the Big Key Ranch."

"Oh." Ellie looked puzzled, then she grinned. "Oh! You mean your parents are divorced!"

Pam's heart almost stopped. She still hated to think about the divorce, even though she knew Mom was now happily married to David Keyes and Dad was happy living his own life here in Detroit. "Yes," Pam said, her voice barely above a whisper, "they're divorced."

Ellie laughed and looked very smug. "My parents would never get a divorce. They don't believe in divorce. I would never want to live with one parent for a while and then another for a while. That's awful!"

Pam looked down at her sandaled feet. Tears burned her eyes, and she was afraid she'd sob if she tried to speak.

"Well, isn't it awful, Pam?"

Pam nodded.

11

Ellie peered closely at Pam. "What's wrong with you? Why won't you say anything? I want to know how you feel about divorce."

"I don't want to talk about it," Pam said stiffly.

Ellie frowned. She stood quietly for a moment and then elbowed Pam. "Get out of here. I want to practice."

"But it's my room for now."

Ellie glared at Pam. "I said get out!"

Pam sucked in her breath and stiffened her back. "This is my practice time, Ellie Pepper!"

"But you're going to let me have the room." Ellie stabbed Pam in the arm with her finger. "Right, Pam? I get the room now!"

Pam wanted to run, but she stood very still. "I won't give it to you."

"You'll be sorry if you don't," Ellie said in a threatening tone.

Pam looked right at Ellie. "You get out right now before I call Mr. Greene."

Ellie stuck her tongue out at Pam.

"You want me to call him?" Pam walked toward the door. She knew Ellie was afraid of Mr. Greene, the man in charge of the music and bookstore. Last week Ellie had been making too much noise, and Mr. Greene had walked back from the store to tell her to be quiet. He had been very stern and hadn't backed down even when Ellie had burst into tears. After he had left, Ellie told Pam that she hated Mr. Greene. Ellie wasn't used to anyone making her behave.

"You get out of here right now, Ellie, and I mean it," Pam said.

Ellie studied Pam for a minute, then glanced toward the door.

"I *will* call Mr. Greene, Ellie."

Ellie cleared her throat. "You're making a big deal out of nothing."

"You leave right now!" Pam sounded very stern, but inside she was shaking as badly as she had the first time she stood beside the horses on the Big Key Ranch.

Ellie shot another look at the door and finally stomped out. "You'll be sorry, Pam Tyler!" she said, slamming the door hard enough to make the picture on the wall pop out at the bottom and then drop back in place.

Pam sighed in relief and sank weakly onto the bench. She stood her books in place on the piano. The only sounds she heard were the distant moan of an organ and her thumping heart.

She sat with her hands in her lap and stared across the small windowless room at the folding chair in the corner. When she took longer than usual practicing, Terryl would sit on the chair and wait impatiently for her to finish. She always tried to finish quicker just to keep from seeing the boredom on Terryl's face.

Pam knew Terryl wouldn't have been bored with the fight with Ellie Pepper. Terryl liked to be in the middle of everything.

Pam suddenly grinned. "I took care of Ellie myself today!"

With a glance at the wall clock Pam touched the Middle C key. She had to stop thinking about other things and practice.

When she finished practicing, she walked to the door and reached for the knob. It wouldn't turn. She frowned. "What's wrong?" she muttered as she tried the knob again. Then a strange feeling wriggled inside her, and her dark eyes grew big and round and scared.

"Locked in?" she asked, surprised. "Could I be locked in?"

Could the door have locked when Ellie slammed it? Pam shook her head. That couldn't have happened. The door had never locked just because it was slammed.

Pam rubbed her hands down her shorts. Could someone have deliberately locked her in? Surely not! "No one would do that," Pam said out loud. "Not even Ellie Pepper." But her voice sounded uncertain, even to her own ears.

She bent down and studied the knob. It was round and smooth and a shiny gold. All the practice rooms had the same kind of knob. The locks were made to be locked from the outside only.

Her heart hammered hard against her T-shirt. She rattled the knob and shouted, "Open the door! I'm locked in."

Would Mr. Greene hear her? Even if he did, he might think someone was playing a joke. He hated practical jokes as much as he hated noise.

Pam glanced at the wall clock and gasped. It was later than she thought. Mr. Greene would already have locked the store and left for the day! He wouldn't have checked the practice room either, since that was Mrs. James's responsibility.

But she had left early today, making Pam promise to leave before Mr. Greene.

Perspiration popped out on Pam's face, and she hit the door hard with both fists. "Ellie Pepper, you come back here right now and let me out! I mean it!"

Pam stopped, surprised and even a little proud of herself. She sounded forceful and strong, just the way Terryl usually sounded. Terryl would be proud of her. Then the corners of Pam's mouth turned down and giant tears filled her eyes. Being forceful wasn't enough to get her out of this locked room.

"Come get me, Terryl," she said, the words almost choking her. She gulped and wiped away a tear. "Terryl. Terryl, I . . . I need you. I need you now!" Then she dissolved into tears.

TWO
Bus Ride

Terryl lovingly touched the bow to the strings and drew beautiful music from her violin. Someday she'd play before large audiences and people would applaud and shout, "More! More!" She closed her eyes as she played; she could almost see and hear what that would be like. Then she laughed aloud. For a while she'd forgotten that she was in the bedroom that she shared with Pam, not in a concert hall.

Suddenly she stopped playing. Her bow dangled from one hand and the violin from the other. Her eyes widened and a feeling of fear stabbed her stomach.

"Pam," she whispered. She looked around as if she expected to see her twin sister in the bedroom with her. Terryl bit her bottom lip and stood very still. Something was wrong with Pam. She knew it as well as Pam would know if something was wrong with her. Mom had said that it was often like that with identical twins.

In a flash Terryl tucked her violin carefully in the red velvet lined case, loosened the bow and laid it in place, then ran to the living room.

"Grandmother! Grandmother, we have to go get Pam from piano lessons right now."

Terryl stopped short. "Oh no. Grandmother took Timmy for a walk." Timmy was the neighbor boy whom Grandmother watched during the day along with the twins. Terryl bit her lower lip again. Dare she wait for them? A shiver ran down her spine, and she knew she couldn't wait a second longer. Pam was in trouble and needed help.

With a trembling hand Terryl scribbled a note to Grandmother that said, "Grandmother, I went to get Pam. Be right back. Terryl." She propped it on the coffee table and ran for the door. Her apartment key hung securely on a chain around her neck. Dad insisted she wear the key, even though Grandmother came to stay with them if Dad couldn't be home.

In the elevator Terryl leaned back against the shiny bar and silently prayed for Pam. Terryl knew that God was with both her and Pam no matter where they were.

Outside the air-conditioned apartment building the hot July air struck Terryl like a blast from an oven. As she ran around the doorman and dodged several people on the sidewalk, she looked down the block where she and Pam took music lessons. Tall buildings reached high into the sky, and cars zoomed past on the street.

"Pam," whispered Terryl. She blinked back tears as she walked around a group of noisy boys and girls crowding into a school bus. She glanced over and saw a girl with honey-brown hair sitting on the bus. She looked like Pam! Was Pam on the bus?

Terryl started to push her way through the line, but a large hand tightened around her thin arm. She cried out in alarm and stared with fright up at a tall bald man who was wearing a white short-sleeved shirt and gray slacks. "Where do you think you're going?" he said sternly.

Terryl scowled and tried to pull away, but his grip tightened. Her heart raced with fear. "Let me go!" she yelled.

"I'm not taking any more trouble from you little kids. I didn't want to make this trip today, but I'm here and you do what I say! Now, get back in line where you belong!"

Terryl's head whirled. "But I don't belong in line!"

"You can't cut. Those are the rules."

She shook her head. "Let me go right now! I have to find my sister."

"What happened to your name tag?'" he said, ignoring her plea. "Didn't I say to leave it on?"

"I don't belong . . ." By then the boy in front of her stepped onto the bus. She pulled away from the man and leaped up the steps. "Pam! Come here, Pam!" Then the girl she thought was Pam turned her head—it wasn't Pam after all! Terryl's heart sank, and she turned to get back off the bus. But the door closed, and the bus started with a jerk. She fell back and landed in the first empty seat next to a boy about her age.

Terryl jumped up just as the driver pulled the

bus into traffic. The bus jerked, and Terryl plopped back into the seat in an awkward sprawl. She flushed with embarrassment and sat up.

The boy stared at her with a questioning look. He had light hair, hazel eyes, and a dimple next to his mouth. "Who're you?" he asked.

She sighed. "My name is Terryl Tyler, and I live back there."

"I'm Tommy."

"I don't belong on this bus," she said.

The boy chuckled. "It looks like you're on, even if you don't belong."

"I'm going to tell the bus driver to stop." She stood, but Tommy tugged her back down.

"He won't stop. He only listens to Mr. Jenkins or Mrs. Ables."

Terryl peered through the window at the buildings and pedestrians flashing past. A shiver ran down her spine. "Where are we going."

"To tour the airport."

Her dark eyebrows shot up almost to her bangs. "But how will I get back?"

"I don't know. You must be rich if you live in that neighborhood back there. Take a taxi."

Terryl touched her pocket in her shorts. She hadn't brought any money. Dad had always told her and Pam to take money with them in case they had to make a phone call to him or for any other emergency. "I don't have any money," she wailed. She leaned toward Tommy. "Do you?"

"Me? No way. This is a free tour for us poor kids that got nothing to do during the summer."

Terryl's brain whirled with ideas on how to get back home. Then, just as the bus stopped at a red light, she knew how she could get the bus driver to open the door. " 'Bye, Tommy," she said.

"Hey, what're you doing?" he asked.

"Leaving!"

"I hope you make it," said Tommy with an excited laugh.

She lunged for the driver and gasped, "Quick! I'm going to be sick!"

The driver jerked around and glared at Terryl. "What? Don't get sick on me!" In a flash the man opened the doors and she leaped down the steps, looking around frantically. Just how many blocks away was her home?

"Hey! You! Little girl, get back on this bus!" shouted Mr. Jenkins, the bald man who had grabbed her. Terryl stared at him as he jumped from the bus, then she turned and raced away. No one was going to stop her from finding Pam!

THREE
Three Unfriendly Children

Her honey-brown braids flapping and flipping, Terryl raced down the sidewalk toward her apartment. She longed to look back to see if Mr. Jenkins was still chasing her, but she couldn't take the chance. She didn't want to stumble or fall. Her heart was pounding in her ears, and sweat was dripping in her eyes and stinging them.

Then she ducked into a store and gasped for breath. Cool air dried the perspiration on her flushed face and her thin arms and legs. The smell of old and new books filled her nostrils. A man behind the counter glanced her way with a frown, then turned back to his customer.

Cautiously Terryl peered over the display of books and out the wide window. Mr. Jenkins wasn't in sight. Slowly she pushed the door open and stepped outside. She craned her neck for sight of the bus, but it was gone and she relaxed. Maybe Tommy had made Mr. Jenkins realize that she really didn't belong with the group of touring children.

As she walked back toward her apartment, she

knew she had a good story to tell her family tonight at dinner. She'd make sure they knew that she had escaped by using her head. She wrinkled her nose and hurried forward. Actually, she'd seen the same escape pulled off by a boy on TV, and it had worked for him.

She dodged around two women deep in conversation. She shouldn't have any problem getting home. If she got lost, she knew she could easily ask help from a policeman. But she wondered if Pam could ask anyone for help.

Terryl shivered. She stopped with a crowd of people at a traffic light and waited to cross the street. Thoughts of Pam whirled around inside Terryl's head, and she impatiently watched the light. Would it ever change? Pam needed her.

Terryl frowned. Her best bet was to see if Pam was still at the music center.

The light changed and Terryl stepped off the curb just as a small blonde girl did. But the girl's ankle twisted and she sprawled to the street almost at Terryl's feet. The girl wore soiled pink shorts and a stained white T-shirt with three red hearts embroidered on it. Her blonde hair was cut short and needed to be washed. Her wide blue eyes were filled with pain and fear.

"Are you hurt?" asked Terryl, reaching to help her up.

"Don't touch her!" A boy a little older than Terryl shoved Terryl aside. "Keep your hands off my sister!"

Terryl bumped against a man dressed in a blue business suit and he frowned down at her before he strode away. Terryl spun around to face the boy and girl. But instead of one boy she found two boys, one on either side of the girl. They both wore shabby tan shorts and black sleeveless T-shirts. They both had medium brown hair and hostile hazel eyes. "You didn't have to push me," snapped Terryl. "I was only trying to help."

The older boy glared at her. "We don't need help. My brother and I can take care of our sister by ourselves! Come on, Gina and Billy. Let's get out of here."

"She was only helping me, Dennis," said Gina in a tiny voice.

Dennis didn't say anything as he half carried, half dragged his sister across the street.

"You know you aren't supposed to talk to strangers," Billy told her in a scolding tone of voice.

Terryl followed them only because she was heading in that direction. She tried to get around them, but several people blocked her path. She wanted to push her way through to get to Pam, but she knew she was too small to make anyone move aside.

"My ankle hurts, Dennis," Terryl heard Gina say.

"We can't stop to look at it," said Billy with a quick look behind him.

Terryl thought he was looking at her, but she noticed that he was searching the street behind her. She wondered if they were running away from someone. She glanced back but didn't see anyone that looked suspicious.

25

"But it hurts bad," Gina said looking up at her brothers with a pleading face.

"Can't you check her ankle?" suggested Terryl from behind them. "What if she sprained it."

"It's none of your business," said Dennis.

"Leave us alone," said Billy. "We don't talk to strangers."

Terryl pressed her lips tightly together and forced back angry words. She had only wanted to help.

Just then she spotted a break in the crowd and dashed through, thankfully leaving the three kids behind. She stopped at another red light, and recognizing where she was, she decided to take a shortcut through the small park where she and Pam often played. Sometimes their neighbor, Beth, would take them and her son, Timmy, to the park to play when she came home from school. Beth was finishing her degree in communications so that she could work at a TV station. Five-year-old Timmy was Beth's only child. Her husband had died when Timmy was four, and shortly after that they had moved into an apartment across the hall from Terryl, Pam, and their dad. It had taken a while, but now they were all friends—including Grandmother, who didn't used to like children.

Terryl thought about Pam again. She was so worried! If only she knew for sure where she was. She stopped by an empty stone bench and sank down on it. A lonely, lost feeling sent tears trickling down her pinched face.

"Is something wrong, little girl?"

26

Terryl jerked up and knuckled away her tears. She looked up to see a man standing there. He was older than Grandmother and had white hair, a mustache, and gray eyes. He carried a carved wooden cane. Terryl swallowed hard and maneuvered herself to the far end of the bench. "I'm all right."

"You were crying. I want to help if I can." He sat down on the bench and looked at her kindly. He smiled and his mustache moved. "Don't be afraid of me."

Terryl bit her lower lip. "I'm not afraid. I'm just not supposed to talk to strangers."

"You're right, of course. I'm not supposed to talk to strangers either. But I felt bad for you when I saw all those tears. I have three grandchildren whom I've never seen. Since I don't get a chance to help them, I thought perhaps I could help you." He smiled gently, and Terryl felt a little better.

She got up from the bench and said, "I'd better go now. My sister needs me."

The man toyed with his cane. "Were you crying for her?"

Terryl hesitated. "Yes. I'm not sure where she is."

"Maybe she's with your parents," he suggested. Terryl shook her head.

"No. She isn't with my mom because she lives a long way from here."

"What about your dad?"

"He lives right over there." She pointed across the park to the tall apartment building. "We live with him during the summer and with Mom the rest of the time. They're divorced." She stumbled over the word. Would she ever get used to the divorce?

"I think you should go home and give your mom a phone call. That'll make you feel better."

Terryl smiled and nodded. "I do need to talk to Mom. Pam and I talk to her every Sunday afternoon."

"Pam?"

"My sister." Terryl stiffened. "I can't stand here talking. She needs me!"

"Well then, you'd better run and help her. I only wish I could've helped you." The man smiled. "Here, take this. If you ever need a friend, call me." He handed her a wheat-colored card with his name, address, and phone number on it. "My name's Garold Holmes, and I also live in your apartment building—on the ground floor, in apartment number five."

Terryl's eyes widened. "You live in number five? My dad knows you."

"And who is your dad?"

"Richard Tyler—the famous writer."

"Of course! I've known Richard since I moved in last year, but I haven't had the chance to meet you and your sister. Richard said he had twin girls."

"That's me and Pam," Terryl said proudly.

"And what's your name?"

"Terryl. Terryl Ann Tyler."

"Well Terryl, now maybe you can tell me what's

wrong, now that you know I'm not a stranger. Maybe I can help you."

Terryl took a deep breath. She thought for a minute and then said, "I was practicing my violin while Pam was practicing piano at the music center. I got that funny feeling that I always get when Pam's in trouble, and I knew she needed help." Then Terryl told him what had happened to her on the bus. Mr. Holmes nodded and clicked his tongue with concern.

He pushed himself up and leaned heavily on his cane. "Let's go to the music center and see what we can see, shall we?" He smiled at her, and she smiled back.

"You don't have to help me, Mr. Holmes."

"I know, but I want to. Like I said, I never get a chance to help my own grandchildren." He held out his hand. "Let's go find Pam."

Terryl's smiled faded, and she glanced toward the music center. "I hope it's not too late."

four
Free!

Terryl stopped at the door of the music center and looked over her shoulder at Mr. Holmes. She felt as though butterflies were fluttering in her stomach. "I forgot! This is Thursday, and the music center always closes at two on Thursdays. I don't know if anyone will be there." Terryl felt a lump in her throat. "I don't even know if Pam's still there."

Mr. Holmes patted Terryl's shoulder. "Don't borrow trouble, Terryl. Let's just see if she is here."

"It looks so deserted!" Terryl's mouth felt dry with worry.

Mr. Holmes bent down to her. His eyes crinkled at the corners as he smiled. "We won't let that stop us."

Terryl nodded slightly. "You're right. We'll try the side door that we always go in."

"Good idea."

Terryl led the way around the large building. Heat rose from the sidewalk and seemed to burn a hole through her sandals. She stopped at the white door surrounded by red bricks. "The door is sure to be locked." Her hand trembled as she tried the door. "It's unlocked! Oh, my!" She shot a startled look at Mr. Holmes. "That's strange. The parking lot is empty, and I don't hear any sounds from inside the building. Maybe we should leave."

"Are you sure you want to?"

She swallowed hard and stuck her head inside the door. "Mrs. James?" she called softly.

"Let's march in as if we belong here," said Mr. Holmes, and they did so. His cane thumped with authority on the tiled hallway as they walked.

Terryl felt strange walking in, but she followed Mr. Holmes with her head high and her shoulders back. "Pam always practices in Room Ten," said Terryl. She stood very still and looked down the hall. Usually the place was full of people, mostly noisy boys and girls coming and going.

"Well then, let's check out Room Ten," Mr. Holmes replied. His voice was just above a whisper, but it seemed to echo down the hall.

"I'm glad you came with me," Terryl said as she flipped back her braids. "I'll find Pam—if she's here." Terryl ran down the hall and stopped outside the door of Room Ten. She stared in surprise at the locked door. She turned away with a heavy sigh. "Well, I guess she's not here. We might as well go," she said to herself.

Inside the room Pam sat with her head down and tears on her pale cheeks. She had tried over and over to get out, but nothing had worked. She'd shouted until her throat ached. Now, she was tired of trying and tired of shouting.

With a sigh she leaned back. "I just want to go

home," she whispered with a sob.

But how would she get out? Maybe she'd have to spend the night locked in the practice room. Dad and Terryl would worry, and Grandmother would worry, too.

Pam's face puckered up, and she pressed her hand to her mouth to stifle a scream.

Outside the door Mr. Holmes asked, "Is this the room?"

"Yes, but she's not here." Terryl took a step away from the door, then turned back. For some reason she couldn't walk away. She looked at the lock and shrugged. "Oh, well." With a quick flick of the lock she turned it and pushed open the door.

Pam leaped up from the chair, crying. "Terryl! You came! You didn't give up."

"Pam!" Terryl flung her arms around her sister, and they hugged each other.

"I knew something was wrong," Terryl said, pulling back and looking into Pam's face. It was like looking in a mirror. "How did you get locked in?"

"Ellie Pepper." Pam suddenly noticed the man standing in the doorway. "Ellie Pepper did it," she said in a weak voice. She shot a questioning look at Terryl.

"You two girls really are identical twins," said Mr. Holmes as he looked in astonishment from one to the other. "I've seen twins before, but you are exact copies of each other. If Terryl didn't have her hair in braids, I'd never be able to tell you apart."

Nervously Pam stepped closer to Terryl.

Terryl laughed. "Pam, this is Garold Holmes, Dad's friend from apartment number five."

Pam smiled and her eyes lit up. "Hello, Mr. Holmes. I'm glad to meet you. Do you take music lessons, too?"

Mr. Holmes chuckled. "No, I came to help Terryl find you. And I'm happy to meet you, too. It seems that you've both had quite a time."

Pam turned to Terryl again. "You, too, Terryl? What happened to you? Did Ellie Pepper do something to you?"

Terryl rolled her eyes. "Not Ellie Pepper. I'll tell you later. Let's go home—it feels funny being the only ones in this building."

Pam agreed and grabbed her books, then ran to the door. She stood in the hallway beside Mr. Holmes and waited for Terryl to lock the door again. She could smell a mixture of spearmint and after-shave lotion on Mr. Holmes.

"Just who is Ellie Pepper?" asked Mr. Holmes as they walked down the hallway.

"She takes piano lessons here, and she lives in our building," said Terryl.

Pam narrowed her dark eyes and gripped her books tighter. "I'm going to find Ellie Pepper and . . . and make salt of her!"

Terryl laughed and finally Pam giggled. "Come on," said Terryl.

They pushed open the door and stepped out-doors into the bright, hot sunlight. Mr. Holmes clicked a lock on the door and pulled it closed.

Then he tried the door to make sure it had locked.

"We don't want you girls blamed if anything turns up missing," he said as he leaned on his cane and looked down at them. "Now, let's find Ellie Pepper and have a serious talk with her."

"Do you know her?" asked Pam.

"I'm sure I know her parents," said Mr. Holmes. "And they need to know what their daughter has done." He sounded grim, and the twins were glad that it wasn't Dad Mr. Holmes was going to talk to about something *they* had done.

"It's strange that the outside door was unlocked," said Pam. "Mrs. James said that she was leaving early and would lock it."

"Maybe Ellie left it unlocked so she could come back for you," said Terryl.

"Well, she didn't come back."

"Maybe she couldn't," said Terryl.

"We'll find out," said Mr. Holmes. "We'll speak with Ellie and her parents."

Terryl glanced at Pam and grinned knowingly. "Our new friend," she mouthed.

Pam nodded. "Watch out Ellie Pepper! You'll be sorry you locked me in."

five
Ellie Pepper

When they were close to the apartment, Terryl saw Mr. Holmes touch his heart and slow his pace. She glanced at Pam, but she was looking off across the street at a black limo driving past. Terryl twisted the bottom of her T-shirt around her finger. "Mr. Holmes, do you want to go home? Pam and I can take care of Ellie Pepper."

Mr. Holmes smiled down at Terryl. His face was pale, and he had a pinched look around his mouth. "I'll be all right, Terryl. I just have to walk slower. My old heart can't keep up with your young legs."

"Grandmother always says that, too," said Pam with a laugh.

Terryl walked slower, and a blast of hot wind blew against her, making her long to run to the cool, air-conditioned building where they lived. "Do you know our grandmother?" she asked Mr. Holmes.

He lifted one white brow. "Your grandmother Tyler? I've met her on a couple of occasions, but I don't know her well."

"Grandfather Tyler died a long time ago, so she doesn't have a husband," said Pam. She walked backward a few steps and studied Mr. Holmes. "Do you have a wife.?"

"She died just before I moved here." Mr. Holmes' voice broke. "I sold our house and moved here because I was too lonely living by myself."

Terryl touched his hand on top of his cane. "We'll be your family, if you want. We'll try to keep you from being lonely."

"Thank you," he said smiling. Terryl caught a sparkle of tears in his eyes before he turned his head. "I'd like that." Then he cleared his throat. "This wasn't a very good day for you two, but it's been a wonderful day for me. I'm glad to have two new friends . . . granddaughters."

"Don't you have grandchildren?" asked Pam.

"Yes, I have three, but I've never . . . seen them." He brushed a wrinkled hand across his lined face. Terryl slipped her hand in his and looked up at him, her eyes full of sympathy.

"Do they live too far away to visit you?" she asked.

He shook his head. "It's a long, sad story and I don't really want to tell it now. Maybe you girls can visit me some rainy afternoon, and we can talk."

Terryl squeezed his hand. "We'd like that."

"We would," Pam agreed.

A few minutes later Pam led the way into the cool lobby, with Terryl and Mr. Holmes right behind her. There was a large couch on an Oriental rug in the middle of the room. A glass coffee table sat in front of the couch, and two end tables stood on either end. A man reading a newspaper sat on a winged chair across from the couch. Soft music played in the background. It was totally different from the house at the Big Key. Even the noises were different. At the Big Key dogs barked, horses neighed, and neighbor children shouted and laughed. Pam tugged her T-shirt over her shorts. Here she and Terryl had to act as if they were in a library.

A quick movement across the room caught Terryl's attention. She stopped and frowned as she watched Dennis and Billy, the two boys she'd run into earlier, pull Gina out of sight behind a large grouping of plants. What were they doing here? Had Fred, the doorman, let them walk right past him into the lobby? He usually kept everyone out that didn't belong. Terryl's eyes widened. Maybe the kids belonged here. But she shook her head—they looked too ragged and dirty to belong in their expensive apartment building.

"Come on, Terryl," said Pam, holding the elevator door. "What are you looking at?"

"Just those kids," she said.

Pam glanced around. "I don't see any kids."

Terryl shrugged. "It doesn't matter." Right now they had to take care of Ellie Pepper. Maybe later she'd have a chance to see what those three strange kids were up to.

When the doors opened Terryl and Pam followed Mr. Holmes out of the elevator and down the carpeted hallway to apartment 999. Terryl bit her lower lip. Pam's heart thudded so loud she was sure the others heard it. They had never been on the nineth floor before. They always rode from the lobby up to the twelveth floor to Dad's plush apartment. Dad had told them that all the apartments were big and beautiful, but he'd chosen the top floor because of the privacy and the view—he liked to see the city lights. Mom had hated the apartment. She'd always wanted to live in the country with a big lawn and garden and lots of animals.

Suddenly Pam stopped. "Maybe we shouldn't talk to Ellie and her parents," she said uncertainly as she laced her fingers together. "I'll talk to Ellie alone another day."

"Ellie Pepper didn't just play a simple joke on you, Pam," said Mr. Holmes. "She locked you in, and you might've been there all night long if it hadn't been for Terryl. We can't let it go."

"He's right, Pam." Terryl jabbed the doorbell. She faced the door with her lips clamped shut and her eyes narrowed.

Pam trembled. "I don't want to do this," she whispered nervously. It would've been better to face Ellie in the music room another day and tell her off.

Mr. Holmes rested his hand on Pam's shoulder and smiled down at her. "I'll take care of this. Don't you worry about a thing."

Pam managed a smile at him just as the door

opened. Ellie Pepper stood there with her hands on her hips and a scowl on her face. Behind her the TV blared out a soap opera. The place smelled of burnt toast and popcorn. Ellie stared right at Pam. "Well?"

"I want to speak to your parents," said Mr. Holmes. He sounded determined.

"They aren't here." Ellie said. She didn't take her eyes off Pam.

"You locked me in," said Pam.

"So?"

"It was a mean thing to do," said Terryl.

Ellie shot a look at Terryl and stepped back half a step. "So?"

Mr. Holmes cleared his throat. "When will your parents be home, young lady?"

"I don't know and I don't care." Ellie pushed on the door, but Terryl blocked it from closing, putting both hands against it. "What do you think you're doing?" Ellie demanded.

"We haven't finished," said Terry with a scowl.

"Who's watching you now?" asked Mr. Holmes.

Ellie frowned. "I'm watching myself."

Pam touched the key hanging on the chain around her neck and saw the key around Ellie's neck. People called them latchkey kids, but she and Terryl weren't really latchkey kids any longer, now that Grandmother took care of them while Dad was busy. "Where's your brother?" she asked Ellie.

Ellie shrugged. "Who knows? Steve was gone when I got home."

41

Pam knew Steve was thirteen, and he didn't like to be bothered with Ellie—or with anyone younger than himself.

"We'll come inside and wait for your parents," said Mr. Holmes.

The twins gasped, and Ellie shook her head hard.

"What's wrong?" asked Mr. Holmes.

"I can't let anyone in when I'm here alone. No one!" cried Ellie. She looked ready to burst into tears, and Pam suddenly felt sorry for her.

"We can't go in," said Pam. She knew how it was at her apartment. Her dad always told them never to let strangers in while he was gone. She looked helplessly up at Mr. Holmes. "Dad will scold us if we go inside."

"He will," said Terryl. She knew they couldn't visit anyone unless the parents were home. "Latchkey kids aren't even supposed to open the door when they're home alone."

"All right, I'll let it go for now," said Mr. Holmes. He leaned down to Ellie and looked her square in the eyes. "But I will be calling your parents later on today. You can count on that."

Ellie suddenly grew pale and bit her bottom lip, but she didn't back away.

Pam shook her finger at Ellie. "You shouldn't have locked me in the practice room. You did a very bad thing. You're in big trouble now."

Ellie lifted her chin. "Who cares?" She jabbed Terryl's arm with her finger. "Get away from my door!" Terryl stepped back, and Ellie slammed the door hard.

"She's not very nice," said Terryl.

"I don't like her," said Pam.

"I think I'd better go home and rest," said Mr. Holmes, leaning heavily on his cane.

Terryl turned to look at him, and her eyes grew wide with fear. "Are you sick?"

Pam licked her suddenly dry lips. "You look sick."

Mr. Holmes shook his head. "I'll be all right. Can you girls get back to your apartment by yourselves?"

Terryl nodded and Pam said, "Yes."

At the elevators Mr. Holmes stepped awkwardly into the down elevator, and Terryl and Pam waited for the up elevator. Then Terryl saw the pinched look on Mr. Holmes' face. She grabbed Pam's arm and tugged her into the down elevator just as the doors were closing.

"We want to walk you to your apartment," said Terryl with a grin.

"That's not necessary," Mr. Holmes said, still leaning heavily on his cane.

"We want to do it," said Pam, eyeing Mr. Holmes with concern. She moved from one foot to the other. What if Mr. Holmes fainted right at her feet? She shivered and pushed the terrible thought aside.

On the first floor the twins walked Mr. Holmes to his apartment. Terryl eased his key from his shaking hand and unlocked the door.

Pam peeked inside to see a room full of books and art objects. A huge silver sofa sat against one wall flanked by chairs and tables. A rocker with a newspaper folded on the wooden seat sat in front of a brick fireplace. A tall marble statue of a Siamese cat stood beside the rocker.

"Shall I get you a glass of water?" asked Terryl as she walked with Mr. Holmes to his rocker.

He sank down, propped his feet on a maple footstool, and sighed heavily. "I didn't know I was this worn out. I do think I'd like a glass of water, thank you. The kitchen's through that door." He waved his hand toward a doorway near a floor to ceiling bookcase filled with books, then dropped it to the arm of the rocker as if it weighed too much for him to support.

Terryl ran to the kitchen, found a glass, and filled it with water. She dropped in two ice cubes from the white refrigerator, and her heart thudded almost as loudly as the hum of the air conditioner. She was afraid that Mr. Holmes was going to drop over with a heart attack, just like a man on TV had done. She trembled, and the water almost splashed over the glass.

In the living room Pam sank to the edge of the sofa and wrapped her arms around her knees. "I don't know what to do to help you, Mr. Holmes."

He smiled weakly. "You don't have to do anything, Pam. I'll be fine after I rest a bit."

"Are you sure?"

"Very sure. I just walked more than I'm used to." He tapped his chest over his heart. "I had a little repair work on this a few months ago, and I'm still getting my strength back."

Terryl brought him the glass of water. "Here, Mr. Holmes. I put in some ice cubes."

"Thank you," he said, then drank the water. "That was good. You girls run to the kitchen and find something for yourselves. There's some iced tea in the refrigerator. I think there's milk, too, if you want that."

Terryl shook her head. "Now that we know you're all right, we have to get home. Grandmother will be worried about us. Come on, Pam."

Pam jumped up. "We'll come see you tomorrow."

"I'd like that," said Mr. Holmes. He tried to stand, then settled back down. "You girls see yourselves out, will you? I need a few more minutes in my favorite chair." He smiled and they smiled back.

"See you tomorrow," said Terryl.

" 'Bye," said Pam. She closed the door gently and faced Terryl. "Well?"

"Well what?" But she knew just what Pam was thinking. "He'll be all right, Pam. He said he would be." Terryl turned away and whispered, "He has to be."

six
A Fight in the Lobby

"I don't want him to die," said Terryl, glancing back at Mr. Holmes's door.

"Let's pray for him," said Pam. "That's what Mom would tell us to do. She said God always wants to help us. We know that, right?" Pam caught Terryl's hand and Terryl nodded.

"Heavenly Father," she prayed, "thank you for taking care of our new friend, Mr. Holmes. Give him rest and strength. Help us to be good friends to him. In Jesus name, amen."

Terryl smiled and squeezed Pam's hand. "He'll be all right."

"He's nice. I'm glad we got to meet him." Pam walked toward the elevators, then she frowned. "Terryl, I don't want him to talk to Ellie's parents."

"Why not?"

Pam shrugged.

"Mr. Holmes only wants to help," Terryl said.

"But I can take care of Ellie myself," Pam said stubbornly.

"You can?" Terryl smiled proudly at Pam. Before they had accepted Christ into their lives Pam had let Terryl make all the decisions and take care of all the problems. Now she was learning how to be strong and how to let God help her take care of her own problems.

Just then Terryl caught sight of Dennis peeking out through a nearby door. He saw her, frowned, and stepped forward with his fists doubled. His brown hair hung too low on his forehead, and his T-shirt had a fresh smear of dirt across it. Billy followed him, then Gina. With a smile, Gina waved a tiny wave at Terryl.

Terryl smiled at her and lifted her hand in a wave.

"Why are following us?" asked Dennis gruffly.

"Yes, why?" asked Billy.

"Are you following us?" asked Gina with her head tilted and her eyes wide.

"What's going on here?" asked Pam, looking from the three children to Terryl and back again.

"Two of you!" cried Gina. She pointed at them. "Look, Dennis and Billy! Two of them!" Gina giggled with her hand at her mouth. Her blonde hair was spiked up around her head, and her blue eyes were wide with wonder.

"Don't talk to strangers," snapped Billy, jabbing Gina in the arm.

"Ouch!" Gina rubbed her arm. "Stop that, Billy. You're not my boss!"

"Don't start fighting again," said Dennis, catching each one by the arm. He stood them on either side of himself and faced Terryl and Pam. "I want to know why you're following us."

"Me?" asked Pam, touching her hand to her chest.

"I'm *not* following you," snapped Terryl. She pointed her finger at Dennis. "And *you* don't have to talk so mean!" She took two steps forward and stopped with her arms folded over her chest. "Just what are you doing here in the lobby of our apartment anyway? Do you live here?" She stepped forward one more step and saw the color wash over Dennis's face. Billy looked startled, and Gina still wore the same look of wonder. "Well," Terryl pressed, "do you live here?"

Dennis took a deep breath. "It's none of your business!"

Pam tugged at Terryl's arm. "Where did you meet these kids?"

"It *is* my business when you start accusing me of following you," said Terryl.

"Who are these kids, Terryl?" Pam asked again.

"I didn't want you to help Gina on the street, and I don't want your help now," said Dennis. "Just leave us alone!"

Pam stamped her foot. "Who *are* you?"

Dennis looked at her. "It's none of your business."

"None of your business," said Billy.

But Gina turned to Pam with a smile. "My name is Gina. And this is Billy and this is Dennis. We're looking for our—"

"Quiet!" Dennis grabbed her, clamping a hand over her mouth. She kicked and twisted.

"Stop that!" cried Terryl. She tugged on his arm. "You're hurting her."

"Get away from us!" Billy said angrily, and suddenly he shoved Terryl. She stumbled back and lost her balance, then landed with a thud near the drinking fountain.

"Don't do that to my twin!" cried Pam. She pushed Billy, and he fell back against Dennis. Dennis lost his hold on Gina, and she fell to the floor with a loud wail.

Terryl leaped up, her dark eyes flashing fire. She ran at Dennis. He grabbed one of her braids and tugged. She cried out and kicked, but she missed him. He pushed her, and she fell back with a plop.

Pam flew against Dennis and knocked him down. Billy reached for Pam, and Terryl shouted, "Watch out, Pam!"

Before Terryl could leap on Billy, someone grabbed her arm. She turned her head to shout, but the words died in her throat at the sight of Grandmother looking shocked and stern.

"What is going on here?" Grandmother demanded, looking down her nose at Terryl. Her voice was even more clipped than usual. Every white hair on her head was in perfect order. Her light-weight gray suit with a blue blouse made her look striking and businesslike. Terryl wanted to sink out of sight. Pam jumped up off Dennis and locked her trembling hands behind her back.

"How dare you girls fight!" Grandmother exclaimed. "I have spent the last hour looking for you, worried that something dreadful had happened. And I find you here—fighting! Now, come with me this instant. Your father will have a good deal to say to you both."

"It wasn't our fault," said Pam just above a whisper.

"They started it," said Terryl.

"Silence! We aren't discussing who's to blame. We're discussing the fact that you were actually fighting—fighting in the lobby for all to see!" Grandmother gripped their arms and tugged them to the elevator. "Not a word from either of you until we're in your apartment."

"We did *not* start it," shouted Dennis after them. "She did!" He pointed right at Terryl.

"Don't you dare to try to blame us," called Billy.

Gina looked sad and waved her little hand at them, but Billy pushed her hand down to her side. She scowled at him.

Terryl glared at Dennis, but she didn't dare open her mouth. Grandmother had very little patience with children, even her own grand-daughters. Since she'd become a Christian, she was developing more patience and understanding. But Terryl knew now was not the time to test Grandmother.

A few minutes later Grandmother stood with her back against the apartment door. Terryl and Pam stood in front of her, waiting, barely breathing. Terryl could feel the tension in the air.

Grandmother walked slowly to the couch and sat down. She folded her long, slender hands primly in her lap and leaned forward slightly. "Now, explain to me what happened in the lobby."

Terryl took a deep breath. "Those kids thought I was following them, and they yelled at me."

51

Pam ran to Grandmother's side. "They were awful to Terryl! The little girl wasn't, but the boys were. And Terryl really didn't do anything. Not until she tried to help Gina."

Terryl sank to the edge of the coffee table, saw Grandmother's look, and jumped up to sit on the chair instead. "I didn't want to fight, Grandmother. But I couldn't just walk away."

"All I did was push Billy," said Pam. She hurried on to explain in great detail all that had happened.

Grandmother's face softened. "Girls, I love you both. I'm sorry that I scolded you the way I did. I was so upset that I couldn't find either one of you, and then to find you fighting was more than I could handle." She slipped an arm around Pam and patted the couch for Terryl to join them. "Now, tell me where you were and what happened."

Pam trembled. "You don't want to know, Grandmother."

"Will it upset me?"

"Yes," said Terryl and Pam together.

Grandmother sighed heavily. "Tell me anyway."

Pam told about being locked in by Ellie Pepper, and Terryl explained why she'd left the apartment to find Pam.

Grandmother shook her head. "That girl should be ashamed of herself! I believe I'll have a word with her parents." Grandmother stood up just as a key turned in the lock and the door opened.

Richard Tyler stepped into the apartment, looking well-groomed and pleased with himself. He was short and slight and very handsome. As he smiled, laugh lines spread from the corners of his dark eyes to his dark hair. "Hello, family. I feel in the mood to take us out for dinner. Anyone interested?"

Terryl and Pam looked at each other, then at Grandmother. Terryl twisted her toe in the carpet, and Pam locked her hands behind her back.

"What's this?" asked Richard, surprised at the lack of response to his announcement. He ran a hand over his dark hair. "What's going on—or will I regret asking that question?"

Terryl ran to him and, flinging her arms around him, hugged him hard. She could smell his after-shave. "We met Mr. Holmes today, Dad."

"You did? Good. He's a nice gentleman." Richard lifted an eyebrow and waited. "What else? Come on. Out with it."

"Tell him," said Grandmother. "Richard, you won't believe what that little Pepper girl did to Pamela."

Richard held out a hand to Pam. "Pam?"

She clutched his hand tightly, "Dad, it really wasn't that bad. I thought it was at the time, but now I don't think so."

"Let me be the judge of that," he said.

Pam took a deep, trembling breath. In an unsteady voice she told the story again with Terryl adding her part and Grandmother commenting now and then.

"Pam said she was going to make salt out of Ellie Pepper," said Terryl with a giggle. "Get it, Dad? Salt—out of Pepper?"

Frowning, Pam jabbed Terryl in the arm.

Richard shook his head and looked very grim. "I get it." Then, with a hint of anger in his eyes, he turned toward the door and said firmly, "I'm going to have a serious talk with that young lady and her parents—right now. Let's go!"

"I want to be in on this, too," said Grandmother. "No one can lock my granddaughter in a room and get away with it!"

Terryl and Pam looked at Grandmother in surprise.

Richard hugged his mother and laughed. "You tell 'em, Mother."

Grandmother stepped back, flushed. But Terryl knew she was pleased by Richard's hug. It was only lately that they had been able to express their feelings of love to each other. Only since Grandmother had become a Christian.

The doorbell rang. Pam squealed and Terryl jumped. Richard frowned at them and turned to open the door.

Beth stepped inside, smiling, and Timmy dashed past his mother and flung his arms around Grandmother's waist. Beth looked cool and pretty in her white and pink summer dress with pink sandals. Pam thought her blonde curls almost looked like a halo around her face. Beth smiled shyly at Richard, then looked quickly away, but Terryl and Pam didn't miss a thing.

They wanted Beth to fall in love with Dad and marry him. They liked Beth a lot more than they liked that model, Briana Jarvis, who their dad was dating. Richard smiled at Beth as she invited them all to her apartment for dinner.

"We have some important business to take care of right now, Beth," said Richard. "But you're welcome to go out to dinner with us afterward."

Beth smiled brightly. "I'd . . . we'd like that!" She turned quickly to the twins. "I also came to see how you girls are. Your grandmother was very worried about you earlier. I wanted to make sure you were all right."

Timmy caught Terryl's hand and looked up at her with wide blue eyes. "Mommy said we had to make sure you were safe. I thought you and Pam were kidnapped by a pirate."

Everyone laughed and Beth said, "Timmy watched a pirate movie a while ago. It made his imagination run wild."

"Did a pirate steal you, Terryl?" asked Timmy. "Pam, did you have to walk the plank?"

Terryl squeezed Timmy's hand. "No, a pirate didn't steal us. We were outdoors."

"And we're OK," said Pam. She bent down and kissed Timmy's cheek. "I think we should go to dinner now, don't you? I'm hungry."

"Can we have pizza?" asked Timmy.

"With extra cheese?" asked Terryl. She knew Dad was still thinking about what had happened to Pam, but she knew Pam wanted all of them to forget it.

Richard shook his head. "We won't think about dinner yet. Mother, stay here with Beth and Timmy. The girls will go with me."

Pam sighed heavily and looked helplessly at Terryl, who shrugged and followed Dad to the door.

SEVEN
Ellie's Parents

"Dad?" Terryl looked up into her father's set face as the elevator dropped to the ninth floor.

"What?" he answered absentmindedly, staring up at the numbers.

"Mr. Holmes wasn't feeling very well when we left him."

"But we prayed for him," said Pam.

"I'll check with him after we see the Peppers," said Richard. "I'm sure he'll be all right. He knows his limitations."

The elevator doors opened before Terryl could ask Dad what he meant. Terryl and Pam followed their father out onto the thick carpet. Terryl noticed some fresh flowers in a huge vase beside a gold framed mirror. Just then the door to the stairs opened, and Dennis, Billy, and Gina stepped through.

"You again!" cried Terryl, dashing forward.

Dennis jerked open the door again and pushed Billy and Gina back through. "Stop following us!" he shouted before the door closed after him. Terryl stopped abruptly.

"What was that all about?" asked Richard.

"Those are the kids we were fighting with in the lobby," said Pam.

"We don't know who they are or where they belong," said Terryl.

Richard sighed. "And I thought we had good security in this place! What else is going to come up?"

Terryl and Pam looked at each other and shrugged.

Richard strode to the Peppers' apartment and knocked. He glanced over his shoulder and motioned for the twins to hurry.

The door opened, and a tall man with dark hair and eyes stood there. He wore blue dress pants and a white shirt that was unbuttoned at the neck. "Yes?"

"Mr. Pepper?" asked Richard.

"Yes."

"I'm Richard Tyler from 1212, and these are my daughters, Terryl and Pam. I've come to talk to you about Ellie."

Terryl peeked around the man and saw Ellie standing beside the couch, her face white and her eyes wide with fear.

Pam wanted to turn and run for the elevator. She didn't like her father to make a scene.

Mr. Pepper glanced over his shoulder, then turned back. "Come in." He sounded tired. "I'll get my wife."

"I'll get her," said Ellie. She dashed away as if she was glad to get out of the room.

"Please, sit down," said Mr. Pepper.

Richard sat on the long, flowered couch with

Terryl on one side and Pam on the other. The smell of roast beef drifted in from the kitchen.

"Just what did Ellie do this time?" asked Mr. Pepper as he leaned back in his chair and crossed his long legs. "No, don't tell me yet. My wife will want to hear this, too."

Pam slid closer to Dad until her leg and shoulder touched him. Then she felt a little better.

Mrs. Pepper walked in, a watchful expression on her attractive face. Her dark hair hung down to her slender shoulders. Her yellow dress pressed against her long legs as she walked across the room. "Ellie said you wanted me, Ed."

"Come sit down, Dena. This is Richard Tyler and his daughters."

Dena Pepper sank to the chair beside her husband's. "Richard Tyler, the writer?"

Richard nodded.

"I'm glad to meet you. I love your books."

"Thank you." Richard cleared his throat. "But we didn't come about my work. We came to talk about Ellie."

Dena frowned questioningly. "Ellie?" She glanced back and motioned for Ellie. "Come sit beside me, Ellie."

"What have you been up to, Ellie?" asked Ed impatiently.

Ellie shrugged and sat down on the arm of her mother's chair.

Terryl could see Ellie was eating up all the attention that she was getting.

Richard leaned forward. "Ellie locked Pam in one of the practice rooms at the music center."

"Ellie!" cried Dena.

"Ellie, Ellie," said Ed, shaking his head.

"I won't do it again!" cried Ellie. "I was angry at Pam, and I didn't know what I was doing."

Pam bit her lip to keep from shouting at Ellie. Pam didn't want this meeting to go on any longer. She wanted to go home and forget what had happened.

Terryl moved restlessly. She felt sure that Ellie was going to get off without any kind of punishment. She looked right at Ellie, who looked back for a second, but then turned her head to hide her face against her mother's arm.

"She had better not do it again!" said Richard sternly. "That was a dangerous thing to do. And a cruel thing."

Ellie trembled at the sternness in Richard's voice.

Ed Pepper pushed himself up. "Ellie really doesn't mean any harm with her little pranks, Mr. Tyler. We'll see that she doesn't do anything like this again."

"She really is a kind, precious girl," said Dena, defensively, patting Ellie's head. "She won't be unkind to your girls anymore—or to any other children."

Richard stood up and walked toward the door, and Ellie's parents walked with him. Ellie stayed behind, then made a face at Pam and stuck her tongue out at Terryl.

Terryl doubled her fists at her sides. Pam looked at her and shook her head.

"We could be friends, Ellie," said Pam.

Ellie rolled her eyes. "Sure."

Just then someone knocked on the door. Ed opened it to find Mr. Holmes standing there.

"Garold," said Richard in surprise.

"Richard, I see you beat me here." Mr. Holmes stepped inside. The color was better in his face, and he was breathing normally. He smiled at Terryl and Pam.

"Mr. and Mrs. Pepper, this is Garold Holmes. He helped my girls today," said Richard.

"And I came to tell you that your daughter needs a good, sound spanking. If you don't have the heart to do it, I'll take her over my knee myself." Mr. Holmes shook his finger at Ellie. She squealed and jumped behind her mother.

"Don't let him hurt me, Mommy!"

"He wasn't going to harm you," said Ed. He turned back to Mr. Holmes. "She already said she was sorry and that she wouldn't do it again."

Pam frowned. She hadn't heard Ellie say anything about being sorry.

Mr. Holmes thumped his cane. "That was a terrible thing to do!"

Richard reached over and touched Mr. Holmes's arm. "Careful of your blood pressure, my friend. Thanks for your help, but this is settled for now."

"I am very sorry that you had to bother with this," said Dena Pepper, "but I'm sure we all realize how children can be." She opened the door wide. "Good evening."

Terryl walked past Ellie, who reached out and pinched Terryl on the arm. "Ouch!" she said, her eyes blazing. Terryl spun to face Ellie.

"What?" asked Ellie innocently. "Did you stub your toe or something?"

Terryl pressed her lips tightly together and narrowed her dark eyes.

"Don't do anything," whispered Pam to Terryl. "Let's just go."

Terryl nodded.

"Did you hurt yourself?" asked Dena in concern.

Terryl glared at Ellie.

"She's all right," said Pam, pushing Terryl toward the door.

Terryl looked back at Ellie. "You'll be sorry," she mouthed.

Ellie grinned and shrugged, and Terryl wanted to slap her.

A few minutes later they stood outside the elevator and Richard said, "Garold, we're going out for dinner. Would you like to join us? We'd love to have you."

Mr. Holmes stroked his mustache and nodded. "It will be better than sitting at home alone."

The elevator slid open and they stepped inside.

"I think you should keep an eye on that Pepper girl, Richard," said Mr. Holmes. "She wasn't sincere at all."

"I won't allow my girls to be around her," said Richard.

Music played in the background as the elevator rose. Richard and Mr. Holmes talked together.

"She pinched me," whispered Terryl to Pam.

"She's mean," said Pam. "Does it still hurt?"

Terryl rubbed her arm. "I guess not."

"Let's forget about Ellie for tonight." Pam tucked her hair behind her ears. "I wonder where those three kids belong?"

"I do, too. I should get them together with Ellie. They wouldn't let her get by with anything." Terryl giggled.

The elevator door slid open and they walked out and down to their apartment. Fresh flowers sent out a pleasant aroma. Then Pam's stomach growled, and she realized that she was hungry. Terryl's brain spun with ideas for getting even with Ellie, then she sighed softly. She knew Jesus didn't want her to get even—he wanted her to love Ellie. But was that possible?

Richard unlocked the door and stood aside for the twins and Mr. Holmes to walk in first.

"Mr. Holmes! Is that really you?" cried Beth in surprise. "I'm so glad to see you!"

"Do you two know each other?" asked Richard.

Timmy stepped close to Richard and slipped his hand in Richard's. Richard smiled down at him and he smiled back.

Mr. Holmes stared at Beth for several seconds. "Beth? What a shock! Beth Harris?"

"Yes! It's been a long time!" She hugged him and kissed his cheek. "A long time."

"It has at that." He held her hand and looked at her with tears in his eyes. "I was sorry to hear about Gabriel."

Terryl shot a look at Dad and saw a strange expression on his face. She wanted to jump inside his mind and read it.

Beth blinked back a tear. "Thank you. He went to live with Jesus."

"So did my dear wife, Selma."

"I heard. I tried to get to the funeral, but I couldn't." She looked around the room as if she suddenly realized where she was. "What are you doing here? Do you know Richard and the twins?"

Mr. Holmes nodded. "I do. I live here in apartment number five."

"You do? How wonderful! I live in 1210. My uncle, Max Palmer, owns this building. He said I could live here until I'm finished with school." Beth hugged Mr. Holmes again. "I am so glad to see you! You remember Timmy? He's no longer a baby."

Timmy stepped forward. "I'm five, almost six. My name is Timothy Palmer Harris."

Pam laughed.

Mr. Holmes shook his head and chuckled. "My, but you have grown."

"I'm this big," said Timmy, holding his hand on top of his head.

Terryl giggled. It was fun to watch and listen to Timmy.

"You certainly are," said Mr. Holmes, laughing.

Beth turned to face Richard. "Mr. Holmes and I once were neighbors."

"How nice," Richard said stiffly. "I had no idea you two knew each other."

"He's the one who got me interested in TV work," said Beth.

"I knew she would be good," said Mr. Holmes.

"Richard and I are neighbors now," said Beth.

"We want Beth to be part of our family," said Pam.

Beth blushed and glanced at Richard.

"We love Beth and Timmy both," said Terryl.

"Yes, we do," said Richard, but he wouldn't look at Beth.

Terryl and Pam glanced at each other and grinned. Maybe there was hope after all!

"I'm happy that we met again, my dear," said Mr. Holmes, hugging Beth close again. "We have so much catching up to do."

"You can both talk over dinner," said Richard. "Garold is going to join us." Richard looked around the room. "Where's Mother?"

"She went home," said Beth. "She said to call her and she'd meet you at the restaurant."

"She wanted to change her clothes," said Timmy.

"Talking about changing clothes," Richard said, turning to the twins. "Will you girls go wash and change into something nice, please."

Terryl wrinkled her nose. Dad had always liked them to dress in skirts or dresses, but Mom had let them wear jeans whenever they wanted.

"Want me to help you choose?" asked Beth.

Both twins said, "Yes," all in the same breath.

Beth laughed and walked them to their bedroom. "I really wanted to hear how it came out with Ellie Pepper."

"Not very well," said Pam.

"Things aren't finished yet," said Terryl with a mischievous glint in her eye. "Not by a long shot," she added under her breath.

EiGHT
Dinner Together

Beth held a flowered cotton skirt out to Pam. "How about this?"

Pam nodded. "I like that. Mom bought that for me." A great sadness filled her, and she was afraid she'd burst into tears. She was glad Terryl was in the bedroom and didn't see her unhappiness.

"I understand, Pam," said Beth softly. She knelt before Pam and gently took her in her arms and held her without speaking.

Pam stiffened, then wrapped her arms around Beth and buried her face in Beth's neck. The smell of Beth's skin and the feel of her arms sent a warmth through her, and finally the sadness slipped away.

She kissed Beth's soft cheek and smiled into Beth's eyes. "I'm all right now."

"Good." Beth kissed Pam's cheek, handed her the skirt, and stood up. "I love you, Pam," she said quietly. "You're a very special little girl."

Pam's heart leaped. "Thanks. I'm glad you're here. It's not as hard with you around."

"I know what you mean." Beth perched on the

edge of Terryl's bed and picked up the rag doll that sat against the pillow. "I'm thankful that God sent you and your family into Timmy's and my life this summer. We needed you, and I think you needed us."

Pam nodded as she slipped on her skirt and pushed her feet into her sandals. "It's funny that you know Mr. Holmes."

Terryl walked in just then. "He's nice, Beth, isn't he?"

"Very nice. I'm glad I found him again."

Terryl pulled on her blue skirt and tucked in her blouse. She kept her back to Beth as she picked up her brush. "He's too old for you to marry, isn't he?"

Beth laughed. "Yes, he is. Besides, I'm not going to get married again for a long, long time."

Terryl whipped around and stared at Beth. "You're not?"

"But what about Dad?" asked Pam, gripped her brush tighter.

Beth flushed to the roots of her blonde curls. "Girls, girls, don't play matchmakers. Please."

"What does that mean?" asked Pam.

Beth slipped an arm around each girl and looked from one to the other. "Don't try to put your dad and me together."

"But we don't want him to marry Briana," wailed Pam.

"She thinks she's going to marry him," said Terryl.

Beth moistened her lips with the tip of her tongue. "Briana's a very interesting person."

"We like her," said Terryl.

"But not for a mother," said Pam. "We want you."

"That's very sweet of you both, but please don't force me on your dad."

Terryl pulled away. "Don't you like him?" She knew when Dad and Beth first met that they didn't seem to like each other at all.

Beth walked around the bed. "Of course I like him. That isn't the point." She laced her fingers together. "I'm not ready for a husband, and your dad isn't ready for a wife."

The twins smiled knowingly at each other and Terryl said, "When you are ready, will you marry Dad?"

Beth threw up her hands. "I give up. Are you girls ready yet so we can go to dinner?"

Several minutes later they sat together at a big table in a quiet corner of a restaurant. Fishnets hung from a stone wall between two huge windows that looked out on Lake St. Clair. Silverware clattered against china plates, and quiet voices drifted across the room. Beth looked dainty and petite between Richard and Mr. Holmes. Pam tried to look grown-up between Grandmother and Terryl. Timmy perched on a booster chair on the end of the table, with Grandmother on one side of him and Richard on the other. Grandmother had wanted it that way.

"How's Winny, Grandmother?" asked Terryl.

"Winny is Mother's wirehaired terrier," Richard told Mr. Holmes.

Grandmother smiled. "He's fine. He wanted to

come, but I told him you girls would be over tomorrow to play with him."

Richard smiled. "I don't know if I'll ever have a great love for dogs like my girls do, but Winny's all right—for a dog."

"We have dogs at the Big Key Ranch where Mom lives," Terryl told Mr. Holmes. "My dog is an old English sheepdog named Malcolm. He's huge and he loves me!"

"And mine is a black cocker spaniel named Sugar," said Pam with a far away look in her eyes. She thought of the fun she'd had with Sugar, and she couldn't wait to see him again.

Everyone was quiet for a moment and Richard cleared his throat. Someone across the room laughed. A waiter hurried past with his tray held high. Richard smiled at the group around the table. "Ready to order yet?" he asked.

"I am," said Grandmother. "I've been hungry for perch."

Mr. Holmes looked at her with interest. "So have I. I believe I'll have perch, too. It's caught fresh daily, and it's delicious. I've had it many times in the past few months that I've lived here."

Beth touched his hand. "I remember how much you liked perch. Remember the time Gabriel caught his limit and you and Selma came over and helped us clean them, fry them, and eat them?" Her voice broke and she blinked back tears.

"I remember," whispered Mr. Holmes. "It was a wonderful time for all of us." He cleared his throat. "Now children, what are you going to order?"

"Big Mac," said Timmy, then ducked his head when everyone laughed.

"A seafood platter would be good for you, Timmy," said Richard, patting Timmy's shoulder. "I remember that you like scallops and shrimp."

Timmy's face brightened. "Yes, I do! That's what I want."

"I'll have the same," said Pam.

"I want the whitefish," said Terryl. Her mouth watered just thinking about it.

"I'll have that, too," said Richard, smiling his special smile at Terryl.

The warmth of his love wrapped around her, and she enjoyed her meal more because of it. It was fun to listen to the others talks and fun to watch the people at the tables around them.

"I want a chocolate sundae for dessert," said Pam as she set her water glass back in place.

Beth laughed. "A girl after my own heart. What about you, Timmy? Do you want ice cream?"

"Cheese cake," said Timmy, watching the waiter walk past with a tray filled with cheese cake.

"Cheese cake for me, too," said Richard.

Terryl frowned thoughtfully. "I guess I'll have Boston cream pie."

"That's for me," said Mr. Holmes.

"Orange sherbet for me," said Grandmother.

A laugh drifted across the room and Terryl stiffened, then slowly turned her head to find Briana Jarvis standing at a table a few feet away.

Terryl jabbed Pam. "Look," she whispered.

"Oh no," whispered Pam. "I hope she doesn't see us."

"She already has. She's coming over." Terryl watched the gorgeous red-headed woman walk to their table and stop just behind Dad. She wore a low-cut blue dress that sparkled when she walked, and she bent down to kiss Richard near his left ear.

"Hello," she said in a low, husky voice.

Richard frowned slightly, then turned his head and smiled. Slowly he stood. "Hello, Bri. Having dinner here?"

"Yes. I see you brought everyone." Briana said, looking right at Beth.

Beth smiled, but didn't speak.

"I don't think you know Garold Holmes," said Richard. "Briana Jarvis, Garold Holmes."

"I've seen your work, Ms. Jarvis," said Mr. Holmes. "Very impressive."

"And I've seen yours, Mr. Holmes. I was sorry when you left TV to retire." Briana shot him her brightest smile. "I didn 't realize you knew Richard."

Terryl listened as Briana chatted on and on. Pam squirmed restlessly.

"We're waiting for dessert," said Timmy when Briana left an opening in the conversation. "Do you want to eat dessert with us?"

Terryl and Pam glared at him, but he didn't notice.

Briana smiled stiffly. "I don't eat desserts. I must get back to my table. Call me, Rich."

"I will." He kissed her cheek and she sailed away, leaving a trail of expensive perfume lingering in the air. Richard sat down and picked up his balled napkin with a quick look at Beth.

"You have a little lipstick on your face," Beth said, her eyes twinkling. She took his napkin. "Allow me." Carefully she rubbed it off and dropped his napkin back in his hand.

"Thank you," Richard said, flushing.

"I'm glad she didn't stay," said Terryl.

Richard frowned at her and she snapped her mouth closed.

Grandmother asked Mr. Holmes about his TV work, and as he told her about it in detail, Pam leaned close to Terryl.

"I'm glad she didn't stay, too," whispered Pam.

"She wanted to. I could tell. She's jealous of Beth."

Pam giggled. "I know."

"Dad hasn't gone out with her in a long time."

"Not since last week. And he used to see her all the time." Pam peeked at Beth. "Beth knows Briana is jealous."

"Beth does like Dad, even if she won't admit it to us," said Terryl. "I think they will get married."

Pam twisted her napkin in her lap. "Do you think Mom would like Beth?"

Terryl chewed her bottom lip and finally nodded. "I think she would."

They looked at each other and whispered at the same time, "I wish she was here right now." But they both knew that she was happy with David at the Big Key Ranch.

Later in the lobby of their apartment Beth kissed Mr. Holmes good-bye and said, "I must get Timmy up to bed. He's had a long day."

"I'm not tired, Mommy." Timmy flashed a smile up at Beth. "You don't need to put me to bed yet."

"Oh yes, I do." Beth caught his hand and walked him to the elevators.

Richard watched her for a while, then turned to Mr. Holmes. "We'll walk you home, Garold."

"Could I offer you a cup of coffee?"

"No, thanks. I must get the twins to bed."

"We're not tired," they said together, then laughed. They sounded just like Timmy, and they both knew they were too grown-up to sound that way.

At the door to number five Terryl said, "Dad, we could go up by ourselves if you want to visit Mr. Holmes for a while." The offer made Terryl feel more like twelve years old instead of ten.

"We don't mind," said Pam. She wanted to feel older, too.

Richard hugged them both. "That's a good idea, girls. I do want to talk to Garold for a while. I'll be up later. No television, now. Get into your pajamas and you may read for a while."

"Yes, Dad," said Pam.

"We will, Dad," said Terryl.

"I hope you girls aren't up to something," said Richard, eyeing them suspiciously.

"Us?" they asked innocently.

Mr. Holmes kissed the twins good-night. They walked to the elevator and Pam jabbed the button.

Terryl listened for the hum of the elevator and the funny noise it made just before the doors opened. She glanced over her shoulder, then froze. "Look, Pam. It's them again."

Pam turned just in time to see Dennis, Billy, and Gina duck behind the plants.

"Let's get them," whispered Terryl.

"But no fighting," Pam said, smoothing her skirt down.

A shiver of excitement slid down Terryl's back as she ran on tiptoe across the lobby to the tall plants.

NINE
Unexpected Help

Terryl crept around the plants, leaned down and said, "Got you!"

Gina squealed and the boys jumped.

"I'm calling the security guard," said Pam from the other end of the plants.

Dennis looked at her with a frightened look on his face. "No! Don't!"

"I'm sleepy and hungry," said Gina. "Dennis, you said we'd have a place to stay tonight."

Terryl stared down at the blonde girl. "Don't you have a place to stay?"

"You talk too much, Gina," snapped Billy, pushing her. She fell back against Dennis and he held her steady.

"Don't fight," said Dennis.

"I should call the security guard," said Pam. But she didn't move. For some strange reason she wanted to reach out and help them. She glanced at Terryl and tried to pass the feeling to her without saying it aloud.

Terryl barely nodded to tell Pam that she knew what she was thinking and feeling. "Do you kids have a place to sleep tonight?" Terryl looked squarely into Dennis's hostile eyes. "Well, do you?"

"We don't," said Gina with a catch in her voice.

Billy jabbed her and she made a face at him.

"Well, we *don't* have a place to stay," she said with tears in her eyes.

"Come stay with us," said Pam before she knew she was going to say it.

Terryl gasped. What would Dad say about three extra kids?

"We can take care of ourselves," said Billy. But tired lines circled his eyes, and they could hear his stomach growl with hunger.

"We do need a place to sleep," said Dennis in a low, tense voice.

"Then come with us," said Terryl. She stepped back and waited for the three kids to walk with her. "We live on the twelveth floor."

"We'll find something for you to eat, too," said Pam. She thought about the food that she'd left on her plate at the restaurant, and she wished that she'd asked for a doggy bag.

Just as they reached the elevator the doors slid open and Ellie Pepper stepped out. "I never saw these kids in the building before," she said, eyeing the three suspiciously. "And I know every single kid in this place."

"They're staying with us tonight," said Pam, "but don't tell anyone."

"They're from out of town," said Terryl.

"We are?" asked Gina. Ellie looked at her.

"I'm Ellie. Who're you?"

The kids looked helplessly at Terryl, and she said quickly, "The oldest one is Dennis and that's

Billy and this is Gina." Terryl edged her way to the elevator and stepped inside with Pam, and the others followed. Quickly she pushed the button for her floor, but before the door closed Ellie jumped inside.

"Oh no," muttered Pam.

Ellie crossed her arms and poked out her chin as she stared at Pam. "I suppose you told them all about me."

"What?"

"They probably already hate me."

Terryl shook her head impatiently. "Ellie, we didn't say anything to them about you. Why should we?"

Ellie sniffed hard. "You're lying, aren't you? I can tell they hate me."

"They don't hate you," said Pam.

"Yes, we do," said Billy.

"See?" said Ellie.

"I don't hate you," said Gina with a smile. "I think you're very pretty."

Ellie flushed and was speechless for a second. "Thank you. You're very pretty, too."

Gina fluffed her mussed-up hair. "I know."

Terryl and Pam giggled. Gina's brothers scowled at her.

The elevator rose quickly. Billy's stomach growled again and his face turned beet red.

"I can't help it. I'm hungry," he said, sucking his stomach in as far as he could.

The elevator stopped and Pam stepped out first. The others followed, even Ellie Pepper. Terryl's hand trembled as she used her key to unlock her door. What would Dad do if he saw them now? Shivers ran up and down Terryl's spine. She let the others walk inside, then she faced Ellie with a set look on her face.

"You can't come in."

Ellie stepped right up to Terryl. "Why not?"

"You just can't."

Ellie tipped back her head. "I'll scream if you don't let me in. People will come running, and they'll want to know what's wrong. When they see you with those kids, I'll tell them that they're runaways."

Terryl knotted her fists. How she wanted to punch Ellie! "All right, come in, but you can't stay long. My dad will be home soon."

Ellie pranced through the door and looked around the room. She spotted the baby grand piano and ran to it. "It's beautiful!"

Terryl ran across the room after her. "Don't touch it! It's my dad's."

Ellie plopped on the bench as if she hadn't heard. She bent over the keys and played "Spinning Song" as well as Dad ever had.

Pam walked from the kitchen where she'd found some food for the kids. "You play so well, Ellie!"

Ellie turned, flushed but proud. "Thanks. I do, don't I?"

"Then why are you jealous of me? I can barely play."

Ellie shrugged, then jumped up. "Mrs. James gives you more of her time and attention. Before you came, I was her favorite student."

Terryl shook her head. "Mrs. James is taking more time for Pam as a favor to Dad."

"That's right," said Pam. "She knows that she'll only have me during the summers, and she wanted to take me as far as possible so that I wouldn't give up piano while I was with Mom."

Ellie looked at them in surprise. "Oh," she said, "I didn't know that."

"You should've asked," said Pam sharply. "It would've saved us all a lot of trouble."

"We'd better check on the kids," said Terryl. She dashed to the kitchen and stopped just inside the door. Gina sat with her head in her arms on the table and she was fast asleep. Billy held his chin in his hands with his elbows propped up on the table. Tears slipped silently down his pale cheeks. Dennis knuckled away tears and jumped up.

"Well, what're you looking at?" he asked gruffly.

"Nothing," Terryl retorted. "Come on. We'll put Gina in my bed so she can get some sleep." Terryl and Pam lifted Gina together and carried her while the boys followed close behind.

In the bedroom, Ellie pulled back the covers and the twins laid Gina down, slipped off her shoes, and covered her up.

"I have a great idea," said Ellie.

"What?" asked Pam.

"Steve is staying with a friend tonight and my mom and dad are gone until about ten. The boys could sleep in Steve's room and leave in the morning before Mom and Dad get up." Ellie looked very pleased with herself.

"What do you say, Dennis?" asked Terryl.

"I guess it would be the best thing." He turned to Billy. "Let's go."

"Are you sure we can trust her?" asked Billy.

Pam had been wondering the same thing. "Can we, Ellie?"

Ellie flung her arms wide and said, "Sure you can. This is a great adventure. And I'm a part of it."

Terryl rubbed her hands down her skirt. Could they really trust Ellie? Dare they? Maybe she'd play one of her mean tricks on the boys.

"We can trust her," said Pam softly.

Ellie smiled, and for just a minute the spark of mischief left her eyes. She turned to the boys. "We'd better go before Mr. Tyler gets here."

Terryl led them to the door. "Ellie, send them up here early. My dad has to be at the university in the morning by seven. We don't want Gina to be afraid when she wakes up and the boys aren't here." Terryl eased the door open and peeked into the hallway. It was empty and she breathed easier.

Dennis walked out, then turned back. "You take good care of Gina. I mean it."

"I will. I promise."

"Don't you dare hurt her or let anyone take her," said Billy.

"Who would take her?" asked Ellie.

"Nobody," snapped Dennis, scowling at Billy.

Billy turned away. "Let's go. I'm sleepy."

Terryl watched them run to the elevator and press the button. She watched until they stepped inside and the door closed, then she raced back to the bedroom.

"She's still asleep," said Pam. "I took off her pink shorts and T-shirt, and she didn't wake up at all."

Terryl and Pam stood beside the bed and smiled down at the small sleeping stranger.

Just then the phone rang in the living room. Terryl slapped her hand over her mouth, and all the color drained from Pam's face.

"Who can it be?" asked Pam.

"We have to answer it," said Terryl. She sped to the living room with Pam on her heels. She scooped up the phone and said, "Hello?"

"Terryl? Pam?"

"Mom!" Terryl turned to Pam with shining eyes. "Pam, it's Mom!"

Pam snatched the phone. "Hi, Mom! It's me. Pam. Oh, Mom, I miss you so much!"

"So do I," said Terryl with her head close to Pam's. She turned and ran to Dad's bedroom and lifted the receiver. "Hi, Mom. I'm on Dad's phone. How's Malcolm? Does he miss me?"

"We all miss you both very much," said Kathleen. "I was thinking about you girls so I decided to call. What's new with you both?"

Pam sank to the nearby chair. She didn't dare say anything about the little girl sleeping in Terryl's bed. "I've been doing well on the piano."

"I've been practicing my violin," said Terryl.

"Did we tell you Grandmother has a dog named Winny?" asked Pam.

"Yes, you told me that Sunday when I called."

"How's David?" asked Pam.

"He's fine. He misses you both."

"And Dani?" asked Terryl. She and Pam both loved their stepsister.

"She's going to be in the horse show next week, and she's been getting ready for that." Kathleen was silent a moment. "Girls, I love you both very much."

"I love you, Mom," said Pam, and Terryl echoed the same words.

"My garden is full of all kinds of vegetables and flowers." Kathleen had always wanted a garden, but never had one until this year. "Sarah came over to watch me work in it, and I gave her a few tomatoes to take home."

Sarah was the girl who lived across the road from the Big Key. She had always caused a lot of trouble for them.

"I miss you, Mom," said Pam.

"I miss you too," said Kathleen. "You'd both better get to bed now. I'll call again Sunday."

"Mom, I wrote you a letter yesterday," said Pam.

"And I sent one out to both of you today," said Kathleen. "Good-bye, my precious girls. Give each other a hug for me."

Terryl hung up slowly and walked to the living room.

Pam looked up and burst into tears.

Terryl slipped her arms around Pam, and Pam flung her arms around Terryl. "Hugs from Mom," they whispered together.

TEN
More Help

Terryl stepped away from Pam, wiped the tears from her eyes with a tissue off the end table, and said, "I'm glad Mom called."

The door opened and the twins turned to watch their dad walk in.

"Sorry to take so long," he said as he slipped off his jacket. "But I wanted to make sure Garold was all right."

"Is he?" asked Terryl.

"Yes, but I know something is troubling him. He wouldn't talk about it. I think Beth might know. Maybe she should talk to him. It was quite a surprise to learn that they were old friends." Richard hung his jacket in the closet, loosened his tie and pulled it off, then unbuttoned his white shirt that still looked crisp and bright. He peered closer at Pam. "What's wrong? You've been crying."

Pam rubbed the back of her hand across her nose. "Mom just called."

"Just now," said Terryl.

"I see." Richard sat on the coffee table and gathered the girls close. He kissed Pam, then

Terryl, then kissed them again. "I know it's hard on you to be away from her, but I couldn't survive if I didn't have you part of the year. I need you and you both need me. We're family."

Terryl rested her cheek against Dad's shoulder and let the warmth of his love spread through her.

Pam pushed her face right into Dad's neck and gradually relaxed, letting his love melt away all the loneliness and sadness.

Finally he held them out from him. "Now, let's get you both to bed."

Pam's eyes widened and Terryl gulped.

Richard studied them for a moment. His dark eyes seemed to read their very thoughts and they trembled. "What's wrong?"

"We can't say," whispered Terryl.

Pam looked pleadingly at Terryl. "I think we should."

Terryl's stomach knotted. "Oh, Pam."

"Oh, boy," said Richard with a heavy sigh. "What have you girls been up to?" He waited, but they didn't speak. "Did you bring a dog in here?"

"A dog?" asked Pam.

"No," said Terryl. "Not a dog."

Richard jumped up and looked around the room. "A cat?"

"Of course not!" said Terryl.

"Oh, Dad," said Pam with a tiny giggle.

Richard peeked under the couch. "A snake?"

Terryl and Pam burst out laughing and shook their heads.

Richard threw up his hands. "I give up. What did you bring home that you weren't supposed to bring? What is the giant secret you want to tell me?"

"Let's tell him, Terryl."

"Should we, Pam?"

"Yes."

"I think you should, too," said Richard. "Out with it."

Terryl twisted her toe in the carpet. "Don't get mad."

"Out with it!"

Pam's heart thudded so loud she was sure it would wake Gina. "Promise you won't call the police?"

Richard slapped his forehead and groaned. "Is it that bad?"

Terryl caught his hand and held it between both of hers. "It's not bad at all, Dad. We're helping someone."

"Helping someone," said Pam.

"Who?"

"A little girl and her brothers," said Terryl.

"Gina, Billy, and Dennis," said Pam.

Richard eyed the girls for several seconds without speaking. Then he said, "Maybe I'd better sit down for this one." He walked slowly to the piano bench and sat down.

They stood before him, side by side, their hands hanging loose and their feet apart. They looked at each other. "You start," they said together. They laughed and said again, "You start."

"Girls, girls. Just start. Give it to me hard and fast, and I'll try to take it like a man." He grinned and they relaxed a little.

"Today I met three kids on the street," said Terryl. "Gina's about Timmy's age, and Billy and Dennis are around our age. Gina fell down and I helped her up. At least, I tried to help her up."

"While she was on the way to help me," said Pam.

Terryl hooked her hair behind her ears and shifted from one foot to the other. "I saw the same three kids different times today. The last time was when we left you with Mr. Holmes at his place."

"They were tired and dirty and hungry," said Pam.

Richard's eyebrows shot almost to his hairline. "And you brought them here? To stay?"

Terryl nodded slightly and Pam said, "Yes."

Richard shook his head. "Where are they?"

"Gina's in my bed, and Ellie Pepper took the boys home to sleep in her brother's room because he was gone for the night."

"What!" Richard looked as if he couldn't believe his ears. "A strange girl is sleeping in your bed?"

"Yes."

"And Ellie Pepper is in on it, too?"

"Yes."

"After what she did today?"

The twins nodded.

"What are you girls going to think up next?" Richard strode across the room. "I want to look at this Gina girl."

Terryl dashed after him, catching at his sleeve. "Don't wake her up."

"She might get scared," said Pam, grabbing his other arm.

Richard walked softly into the bedroom and looked down at the small girl. She sighed in her sleep and turned on her side. Richard shook his head and walked back to the living room with the twins trailing him.

"You will let her stay, won't you, Dad?" asked Terryl.

Richard turned with his hands on his lean hips. "Where are her parents?"

"We don't know," said Pam. "They didn't say."

"But they looked scared," said Terryl. "I think someone's after them."

Richard stabbed his fingers through his hair. "I think you've been reading too many of my mystery books."

"She can stay, can't she?" asked Pam.

Richard looked at them for a moment. "She can stay. But tomorrow we are going to find out who the kids are and get them back to where they belong."

"All right!" cried the twins. They flung themselves against Richard and hugged him hard.

The next morning, while Gina was eating a bowl of cereal with Terryl and Pam, the doorbell rang. Terryl ran to answer it before Dad could. She was worried that he would frighten Dennis and Billy. Richard had called the university for someone to take over for him for the day. Now he was taking a shower and getting dressed.

Terryl opened the door and Dennis, Billy, and Ellie walked in. "Good morning," said Terryl, suddenly feeling very nervous.

"Where's Gina?" asked Dennis.

"Eating breakfast." Terryl led the way to the kitchen. "Did you eat?"

"I fed them," said Ellie. "Marshmellows and raisins. That's what I always eat for breakfast."

Gina looked up from her bowl. Milk lined her mouth. "Hi, Dennis. Hello, Billy."

They stood on either side of her and looked her over as if they were making sure that she was all right. "Hi," they said at the same time.

"Sit down, boys," said Terryl. "Have some melon if you want." She slid the glass bowl of golden melon pieces toward the boys as they sat on either side of Gina.

Ellie reached for a piece and stuck it into her mouth. She plopped down beside Pam.

"We want to know where you kids live," said Pam.

"What do you mean?" asked Dennis sharply.

"You know what she means," said Terryl. "Where do you live and who are your parents and why are you running away?"

Billy jabbed Gina's arm. "What have you been telling them?"

"Nothing." Gina's face fell, and giant tears filled her eyes. "I promised. Didn't I?"

"Leave her alone," said Dennis. He turned to Terryl and Pam. "We'll be leaving here when Gina's finished with breakfast."

"Oh no you won't!" cried Ellie. "I want to hear

all about the mystery you're mixed up in."

"What mystery?" asked Pam, leaning forward, a piece of melon stuck on her fork.

Dennis frowned at Ellie. "There's no mystery. We're here looking for someone."

"For Grandfather," said Gina.

"Gina!" her brothers cried, glaring at her. "You promised!"

Ellie laughed in delight and bobbed up and down. "I knew it! I knew it! Who is your grandfather?"

"Do we know him?" Terryl waited breathlessly.

Pam scooted to the edge of her seat. "Do we?"

The boys looked at each other. Water dripped in the sink. The refrigerator clicked on and hummed quietly.

Dennis took a deep breath. "We don't know who he is."

"What?" The twins and Ellie cried at once.

"That's impossible," said Pam.

"But it's true," said Dennis.

"We want to hear the whole story," said Terryl.

"Me, too," said Gina. "Tell me again, Dennis."

Billy picked up a paper napkin, balled it up, and tugged at it until it lay in shreds on the table.

Dennis leaned back in his chair. "Fourteen years ago my mom had a terrible fight with her parents, and she ran away from home. She got married and had us kids and never talked to her parents again. My dad sent her parents announcements of our births, but Mom wouldn't let him call them. She wouldn't even let him tell us anything about our grandparents. Then we heard that Grandmother had died. Mom cried, but she wouldn't call her dad and talk to him. We never could find out who he was or where he lived. Then one day we drove past this apartment and Dad said, 'Joy, it's time you made up with him. We can stop and you can go in and see him now.'

"Why did you kids decide to come find him?" asked Pam.

"We just did," said Dennis.

"Because Mom and Dad went on a trip last week and won't be back until next week," said Billy. "And Mrs. Mason is mean to us. She slapped me for no reason and sent Gina to bed without her dinner. So we decided we should find Grandfather and stay with him until Mom and Dad come home."

"This is so exciting!" Ellie's eyes danced. "How do you expect to find your grandfather if you don't know his name?"

Dennis moved restlessly. "We thought we could read all the names of the people who live here and look at all the old men and somehow find him."

"We know one old man," said Terryl. "Garold Holmes in number five."

"Do you think it could be him?" asked Pam.

"I don't know. You could find out if he has a daughter named Joy," said Dennis.

"That's easy enough," said Terryl.

"I'll ask him myself," said Ellie. She started toward the door, but Terryl caught her arm and stopped her.

"Don't. If it *is* Mr. Holmes, we have to be careful. He has a weak heart."

Just then Richard walked in. "I see the gang's all here," he said with a cheerful laugh.

Dennis and Billy looked as if they wanted to hide under the table.

"Dad, this is Dennis and this is Billy," said Terryl.

"And Mr. Holmes might be their grandfather," said Ellie.

"What? Impossible," said Richard. "He has no family."

Terryl's heart sank. She'd thought the mystery would be simple to solve. If Mr. Holmes wasn't their grandfather, then who was?

ELEVEN
The Big Surprise

Terryl pulled her knees up to her chin and watched Dad's face as he listened to Dennis tell his story again. The carpet felt soft under her. She pressed her back against the chair that Pam sat in. Dad sat in the chair beside her and the others sat on the sofa. She had tried to get Ellie to leave, but she had insisted that she wanted to see this thing to the end. She seemed to think it was a book or a movie. Terryl forced back the bad things she wanted to say to Ellie as she looked at her.

"That's what happened," said Dennis. He settled back and watched Richard's face.

"We have to find our grandfather," said Billy.

"I can settle this once and for all," said Richard. "I'll call Garold Holmes and ask him if he has a daughter named Joy, who is married to a Rob Hysell. And if he has three grandchildren. I'm sure he doesn't, but I'll ask anyway."

"Do you know anyone else in this building that could be our grandfather?" asked Dennis.

Richard shrugged. "There are a few old enough, but none of them lives alone. And you said your grandmother had died a while back."

"That's right." said Billy.

Terryl trembled. "Maybe it *is* Mr. Holmes."

"Maybe so." said Richard. he pushed himself up. "I'll call from my room. You kids wait here."

As the door closed behind him, Pam bumped Terryl with her knee and mouthed, "I'm praying."

Terryl nodded and silently prayed for the kids and for Mr. Holmes. She knew God loved them and wanted the very best for them. Suddenly she jumped up. "I just remembered something!"

"What?" asked Pam while the others echoed the same.

Terryl locked her hands together in front of her and took a deep, steadying breath. "Mr. Holmes told us that he had three grandchildren that he had never seen. He said some day he'd tell us the whole story. Remember?"

"I remember!" cried Pam, leaping to her feet.

Gina jumped up and down, shouting with glee. Billy and Dennis sat quietly as if they didn't dare believe it.

"That doesn't mean these three kids are his grandchildren." said Ellie.

"Oh," said Gina and plopped back down.

Terryl and Pam shrugged and sat down again, too.

"Do you always have to ruin everything, Ellie?" asked Pam.

"I didn't ruin anything. And don't say I did!" Ellie shook her finger at Pam. "I mean it."

"Is he or isn't he our grandfather?" asked Gina.

"We'll know soon enough," whispered Dennis as he looked toward the door that Richard had walked through earlier.

"I wonder what's taking so long," said Billy, rubbing his hands up and down his thin legs.

Richard walked in, and Terryl leaned weakly against the chair. What was he thinking? She couldn't tell by his expression.

"Well?" asked Billy, his face as white as Richard's shirt.

Richard fingered the knot on his tie. "There's a good possibility," he said thoughtfully, "that Mr. Holmes is your grandfather."

Terryl leaped up along with the others and shouted and cheered as loudly as Gina. Then suddenly the uncertain look on her dad's face stopped her. "What's wrong?" she asked in a shaky voice.

Dead silence fell and all eyes bored into Richard.

"I didn't tell him the kids are here. I didn't know if he could take it." Richard slipped on his suit coat, adjusted his tie again, and tugged on his cuffs. "I'm trying to think of a good way to approach this so that it's not too much of a shock for him."

Ellie stepped forward. "I say just tell him. I'll do it right now."

"Hold it, Ellie," said Richard sternly. "You leave this to me." He looked at Dennis, Billy, and Gina. "Wait here and I'll call you when it's time to go down. Terryl and Pam will walk with you."

"I will, too," said Ellie.

"If you must," said Richard. "See you all later."

The door closed behind Richard, and the sudden silence sent shivers over Terryl. Waiting was hard. Maybe they could do something to keep everyone's mind off Dad's meeting with Mr. Holmes. She glanced around the room and the piano caught her attention. She turned to Ellie. "Will you play for us? You can give a concert right now on the famous Richard Tyler's baby grand."

"Do, Ellie," said Pam.

Ellie hesitated only a fraction of a second, then ran to the piano and sat down. "For my first piece I shall play Kabalevsky's 'Sonatina.'" She struck the first note and Pam held her breath in awe. The music rang gloriously through the room. Just as she finished the third song the phone rang.

Terryl beat Pam to it and scooped it up. "Hello," she said breathlessly.

"Hi, It's Beth."

"Oh, Beth. It's Terryl. We're expecting an important call from Dad."

There was a long silence. "Do you want me to hang up?"

"Yes. Wait, no. I want to ask you about Mr. Holmes."

The others pressed in around Terryl until she almost dropped the phone.

"What about him? And what's all that noise I hear?" asked Beth. "Do you want me to come over?"

"Yes! Please do!" Terryl put down the receiver and ran to the door, flinging it wide.

"What's going on?" asked Ellie, peeking around the corner.

"Beth is coming. She knows Mr. Holmes." Terryl gripped the door tighter as Beth and Timmy walked across the hall.

"Hi, everyone." said Timmy. His light hair looked just washed and blown dry, and he wore jeans and a red T-shirt. He stopped short in the doorway and stared at Gina and the boys. "I don't know you, do I?"

Pam slipped an arm around Gina and introduced the kids to Beth and Timmy.

Beth looked questioningly at Terryl. "What did you want to ask me?"

"About Mr. Holmes," said Ellie.

"Does he have a daughter named Joy?" asked Dennis in a tight voice.

Beth nodded, then looked questioningly at the anxious children. "Yes, he does. But something happened years ago, and she left home and wouldn't return. Mr. and Mrs. Holmes were heartbroken. Why?"

"We're going down," said Dennis, as he pushed through the group and into the hall. Billy and Gina followed.

"Wait for us!" cried Pam, running to the elevator.

"These three are his grandchildren," said Terryl as she closed the door after the others. "We're going to see him now. Want to come?"

"You bet!" Beth caught Timmy's hand and followed Terryl down to the elevator.

"Is this a party, Mommy?" asked Timmy, running to keep up.

"It seems like it," said Beth with a reassuring smile.

Just as they stepped out of the elevator into the lobby a woman walked across the floor, her face grim and her steps heavy. She wore brown slacks and a yellow and black plaid blouse.

"Look!" cried Billy, pointing to her.

"There you are!" she cried, striding toward them. She was tall and big and had a very determined look on her wide face.

"Don't let her get me." Gina jumped behind Pam to hide.

"It's Mrs. Mason," whispered Dennis in horror.

She reached for Dennis, but Beth stepped in her way.

"Don't touch that boy!" said Beth with a voice that rang with authority.

Terryl's eyes widened. Mrs. Mason towered over Beth, but Beth didn't seem frightened at all.

Pam stepped closer to Terryl, keeping Gina at her side.

Mrs. Mason glared down at Beth. "I am in charge of these children, and they are going home with me—right now!"

"Oh, my," said Ellie, stepping close to Terryl and Pam.

"They're here to see their grandfather," Beth said and turned to Dennis. "Knock on the door."

"Don't move a step!" Mrs. Mason reached over and gripped Dennis by the arm.

Terryl started for the door to knock, but Ellie beat her to it.

The door opened and Richard stood there. "This looks like a mob," he said.

"I need help, Richard," said Beth, her face white and her voice strained.

"Come in, everyone," said Mr. Holmes from where he sat in his rocker.

Richard stepped outside into the lobby. "What's going on here?"

"These children are going to their home with me," said Mrs. Mason grimly.

Dennis twisted his arm and broke free and ran into number five. "Are you my grandfather, Mr. Holmes?"

Mr. Homes pushed himself up and leaned heavily on his cane. For a moment he couldn't speak. Then tears sparkled in his eyes and he said, "Well, bless my heart, I believe I am."

TWELVE
The Missing Grandfather

Terryl caught Pam's hand. "Did you hear that, Pam?" Terryl's voice broke, and she blinked back the tears that brimmed in her eyes. "He says he thinks he's their grandfather!"

Gina and Billy pushed past everyone to stand before Mr. Holmes with Dennis.

"Are you really our grandfather?" asked Gina in awe.

Billy jabbed her and frowned. "He said he was, didn't he?"

Pam sniffed hard. "Isn't it wonderful?" She tugged Terryl's hand, and they ran together to stand beside the fireplace where they could see every expression on Mr. Holmes's and the children's faces.

Mrs. Mason brushed Ellie aside and sailed into the room, her face like a thundercloud. "I won't allow these children to stay here!"

"Hey! Watch it!" cried Ellie.

"What's going on?" asked Richard, glancing around with a troubled frown.

Beth slipped her hand in his and looked helplessly up at him. "I tried to keep her away from the children. She says she's in charge of them. She doesn't want them to see Mr. Holmes."

Richard patted Beth's trembling arm. "Don't worry. I'm sure it'll all work out."

"Are you really our grandfather?" asked Gina again as she stepped forward one hesitant step.

Mr. Holmes brushed an unsteady hand across his face. "I think so."

"What did he say? I couldn't hear," said Ellie.

Terryl squeezed Pam's hand.

Mrs. Mason gripped her purse tighter as she marched across the carpet toward Mr. Holmes. "These children are in my care, and I won't have you putting ideas into their heads!"

Mr. Holmes narrowed his eyes into slits of steel. "I don't want you to interfere, madam!"

"Well!" Mrs. Mason puffed up like a roasting marshmallow. "I am leaving—and so are the children!"

"The children are staying with me for now." Mr. Holmes's voice rang with an authority that made Terryl chuckle to herself. She could see Mrs. Mason cringe.

"Yes, the children are staying," Ellie put in.

"Quiet, Ellie," said Richard. "Let Mr. Holmes handle this."

Ellie looked hurt. "I was only trying to help."

Mrs. Mason glared at her, then turned back to Mr. Holmes. "I called the children's parents and told them that the children had run off. I can't be responsible for them if they continue to defy me." Mrs. Mason reached for Dennis, but he jumped away.

"Don't touch me!" Dennis rubbed his hand down his bare arm as if to rub even the thought of her touch away.

Mr. Holmes looked at the woman. "I will be responsible for these children. You may leave."

Mrs. Mason folded her arms over her breast and stood with her back very straight and a determined look on her face. "I will not leave these children here. Mrs. Hysell said to keep the children away from you."

Pam trembled at the sound of the woman's voice.

Mr. Holmes shook his head. "I think it's time my daughter and I resolved our differences. Leave the children with me. Joy can come get them when she returns."

Mrs. Mason frowned. "That's quite impossible! The children must go with me now!"

"No!" they all cried at once.

Gina walked hesitantly up to her grandfather and slowly held out her tiny hand. "I want to stay with you," she whispered.

"And so you shall!" Mr. Holmes sank into his chair and gathered Gina close.

Richard took Mrs. Mason firmly by the elbow and began to guide her toward the door. "I think it's time you left, Mrs. Mason. Mr. Holmes can handle his grandchildren without any interference from you."

With Timmy at her side Beth held the door wide and said, "Please go quietly, and don't cause any further trouble, Mrs. Mason."

"I'm not leaving!" the woman stormed.

"Oh yes, you are," said Richard. He was much shorter than the big woman, but he was determined to walk her to the door.

Terryl puffed out with pride. "That's my dad," she whispered.

Pam grinned at Terryl and nodded.

"My dad could've done that," said Ellie.

"You'll all be sorry for this!" said Mrs. Mason grimly.

"I doubt that," said Richard.

Beth pushed the door closed with a sharp click, then leaned against it and smiled a satisfied smile.

Richard glanced at her and winked and she winked back. Watching them, Terryl and Pam smiled a secret smile at each other.

Gina touched Mr. Holmes gently on the cheek. "Do I call you Grandfather, or what?"

He laughed and blinked away tears. "Grandfather is perfect. Unless you want to call me Grandpa."

"Grandfather," said Dennis.

"Grandfather suits you," said Billy.

"This is exciting," said Ellie.

Terryl rubbed her hands together. "Are they really your grandchildren, Mr. Holmes?"

"It seems so," he said with a smile.

"Will you let them stay here with you always?" asked Pam.

"I don't know," Mr. Holmes said, and his face clouded over with concern.

Richard slipped one arm around Pam and the other around Terryl. "Girls, I think we should get out of here and leave them alone to get acquainted."

"I'm not leaving," said Ellie with her jaw set, and the twins felt the same way.

"I think we all should go," said Beth gently.

"Do we have to?" asked Terryl.

"Stay for a while," said Mr. Holmes. "Please."

"Don't you think you should rest?" asked Beth, gently taking her friend's hand. "You can talk with the chidlren in a little while."

Mr. Holmes settled back into his chair. "You're right, Beth. I am weaker than I thought." He patted her hand, then turned to look at Dennis and Billy in front of him and Gina on his lap. "Children, let me look at you." His voice broke and he cleared his throat.

"Why does he want to look at them, Mommy?" asked Timmy.

"Because he's so glad to see them," said Beth with a catch in her voice and a tear in her eye.

"Yes, I am," said Mr. Holmes.

Gina kissed his cheek. "You look tired."

"I guess I am."

She wriggled off his lap and stood before him. "We'll be quiet so you can rest." She turned to her brothers. "Won't we?"

"Yes," said Dennis.

"For a little while," said Billy.

"I really do think we all should leave," said Richard.

"No," said Ellie. "I want to stay!"

"The children can go home with me until you're rested, Garold," said Richard.

"We'll bring them back in an hour," said Beth.

"I'm staying right here," said Ellie.

The twins frowned at her.

"You're leaving with us," said Richard in a voice Terryl knew Ellie had to obey.

Mr. Holmes smiled at the children. "Gina. Dennis. Billy. I wish I could get to know you right now. All three of you are beautiful. Gina, your mother looked a lot like you when she was your age. She liked pickles more than anything else."

"She still does," said Billy.

"Bread and butter pickles and dill pickles," said Dennis.

Mr. Holmes nodded. "I keep pickles in my refrigerator for her now. I always keep pickles . . . just in case." His voice faded away.

Richard stepped forward. "Now, children, we are going to my placce and give Mr. Holmes a chance to rest.

"Good-bye, Grandfather," said Dennis. "We'll be back soon."

"Good-bye, Grandfather," said Billy and Gina as they walked backward toward the door. Gina waved one small hand.

"Mr. Holmes, do you want me to fix a cup of tea for you before I leave?" asked Beth.

"No thanks, Beth." He squeezed her hand. "Thanks for being here for me."

She bent and kissed his wrinkled cheek. "See you later."

He nodded. "Our prayers have been answered,

Beth. All these years and now they're being answered."

"Praise God," she whispered as she blinked away tears.

Terryl smiled as she walked out the door after Pam.

At the elevator Ellie said, "Look! There's Mrs. Mason!"

"Oh no," said the twins.

Dennis pulled Billy and Gina close to his sides. "Don't let her hurt us."

"She won't," said Richard grimly.

Beth pushed the elevator button. "I'll take the children up."

"And I'll take care of Mrs. Mason." Richard strode across the lobby just as the elevator doors slid open.

"Inside, children," said Beth.

Terryl looked over her shoulder to see Dad as she stepped forward. She saw him stop before Mrs. Mason, and then the elevator doors slid closed.

"She'd better not punch Dad," said Pam.

Beth patted Pam's shoulder. "She won't."

"She's real mean," said Billy, shivering.

Ellie stepped toward the elevator panel. "I think I'll stop at my place." She jabbed the button with the nine on it.

"I thought you were going with us," said Pam.

Ellie shrugged. "I changed my mind."

"Why?" asked Pam.

Ellie poked out her chin and squared her

shoulders. "I can do what I want, Pam Tyler."

"Don't fight, children," said Beth.

Pam bit back the sharp words that wanted to tumble out of her mouth.

Terryl studied Ellie closely. Just what was she up to?

THIRTEEN
Ellie's Prank

"What are you going to do, Ellie?" asked Pam suspiciously. She didn't trust Ellie at all, even if she had been nice to Dennis, Billy, and Gina.

Ellie grinned a secret grin that made Pam even more suspicious. "Why should I tell you?"

Pam grabbed Ellie's arm. "Don't you dare do anything to hurt these kids!"

Ellie pried Pam's fingers off. "Why should I hurt them?"

"You do mean things all the time and you know it!"

"I do not! I was only going to see my mom and dad. They don't know where I am."

"Oh."

Terryl flipped back her braids. "You never cared to tell them before, Ellie. I think you are planning something."

Ellie stuck out her chin. "I am not!"

"Girls," said Beth with a shake of her head.

The elevator opened, and Terryl watched Ellie walk out. "She's going to do something that she doesn't want us to know about," Terryl whispered to Pam.

"I think so, too," said Pam.

The doors slid shut and the elevator rose quickly. A few minutes later Pam unlocked their apartment door and pushed it open. She motioned for Terryl, and they stood side by side until everyone was inside, then she signaled to Beth.

Beth leaned down to her. "What?" she whispered.

"We want to check on Ellie. We think she's going to go back to see Mr. Holmes and make trouble."

Beth sighed and finally nodded. "Come back as soon as you can."

"We will," said Terryl.

They ran to the elevator and rode in silence to the lobby.

"Do you see her?" asked Terryl as she walked away from the elevator.

"I don't. And I don't see Dad." Pam turned all the way around as she looked. She saw two men walk in the front door looking hot and tired.

"Mrs. Mason had better not hurt him!" said Terryl, clenching and unclenching her fists.

"Look!" Pam jabbed Terryl's shoulder. "There's Ellie. What is she doing?"

Ellie stood with her back to the twins, looking around a corner and down a hallway.

"Maybe she sees Dad and Mrs. Mason," said Pam.

"Let's go." Terryl tiptoed with Pam across the lobby, but before they reached Ellie she slipped around the corner and ran down the hallway. The twins looked at each other questioningly, then ran after her.

"Where is she going?" whispered Pam.

"Maybe the storage room," said Terryl. Once when they were seven she and Pam had played hide and seek in the storage room. Mom had spanked them and told them never, never to play in the storage room again.

"That's strange," Pam said.

Ellie slipped inside the storage room without looking back.

"What do you suppose she's doing?" asked Terryl.

Pam held her ear to the door and listened. "I don't hear anything." Cautiously Pam opened the door and slipped inside with Terryl on her heels. Ellie wasn't in sight.

"Where is she?" whispered Terryl.

Pam shrugged, then peered around the dimly lit, crowded room. Dust tickled her nose, and she rubbed it to hold back a squeeze. "I can't see her."

Terryl tiptoed around a large table that sometimes stood in the lobby. She slipped around a pile of cardboard boxes and spied a half-open door that she knew led to the maintenance man's office. She motioned to Pam, and they carefully peeked into the room. Ellie stood at a desk with the phone in her hand.

"Hello, Grandfather," she said in a disguised voice. "This is Dennis. I want to come talk to you now."

Terryl pressed her lips tightly together, and

Pam narrowed her eyes and doubled her fists.

"I'll be right there, Grandfather." Ellie hung up and smiled smugly.

"What do you think you're doing, Ellie Pepper?" demanded Terryl, standing in the doorway.

Pam marched right up to Ellie. "How could you do that to Mr. Holmes?"

Ellie backed away, her face suddenly white. "I wanted to talk to Mr. Holmes, and I knew he wouldn't talk to me or even let me in his door."

Terryl shook her finger at Ellie. "You are mean! Mr. Holmes doesn't feel very well and you should leave him alone!"

Ellie tossed her head. "Well, I won't leave him alone. I want to know what happened to make his daughter, Joy, leave home. I want to know everything, and if I can get inside his place, I won't leave until he tells me. I'm always left out of everything, but this time I won't be! So there!" She dodged around the desk and out the door before the twins could stop her.

"Come back, Ellie Pepper!" cried Pam.

"You stay away from Mr. Holmes!" shouted Terryl.

Forgetting all about the rule of no running in the building, they ran through the storage room after Ellie. She slammed the door shut and Pam struggled to open it. Finally with Terryl's help she opened it, then they ran down the hall and around the corner to the lobby. Ellie stood in front of Mr. Holmes's apartment, her hands on her hips and her face ashen.

Puffing and panting, Pam slid to a stop beside Ellie. "Don't ring the bell, Ellie."

Terryl pushed Ellie aside and blocked the door. "Get away from here. I can't believe you'd be so mean to Mr. Holmes!"

Ellie trembled and pointed a shaking finger at the door. "It's . . . it's too late."

"Too late?" asked Pam with a frown.

A shiver ran down Terryl's back. "Too late for what?" she asked.

"I didn't mean for it to happen," said Ellie with a sob.

"What happened?" asked the twins together.

Ellie shook her head. "It's terrible!"

Terryl gripped Ellie's arm. "What is it?"

"Tell us," said Pam grimly.

"Mrs. Mason is inside with Mr. Holmes."

"Mrs. Mason?" Terryl's stomach cramped with sudden fear. "Why should he let her in?"

Ellie swallowed hard. "I let her in."

"You did?" Terryl shook her head.

"But why?" asked Pam.

Ellie sniffed and rubbed an unsteady hand across her nose. "Mrs. Mason said . . . said that if I got her inside to talk to Mr. Holmes, she would be sure I learned the whole story."

"And?" the twins asked at once.

"And when he opened the door, she pushed right past me and walked in. I couldn't stop her even when I tried. She shut the door—right in my face!"

"Ellie Pepper! Think what a terrible thing you

115

did!" Pam caught Ellie's arm and shook it.

Ellie jerked away. "I didn't mean to hurt anyone, and you know it!"

"Let's get Dad," said Terryl, already on the run to the hall phone.

"But where is he?" asked Pam from just behind Terryl.

"I hope he's home." Terryl lifted the receiver and pushed the buttons. On the third ring Beth answered. "Beth, it's Terryl. Is Dad there?"

"No. He's in the lobby."

"We're in the lobby, and he's not here. If he comes home, tell him to go see Mr. Holmes right away."

"Did something happen to Mr. Holmes, Terryl?"

"No, not yet anyway. Just send Dad. 'Bye, Beth." Terryl hung up right in the middle of Beth's next question. "Dad's not home, Pam."

Pam shivered. "Oh, dear."

"We've got to get Mrs. Mason away from Mr. Holmes before she upsets him too much," said Ellie.

Pam turned on Ellie, her eyes blazing. "It's all your fault. If you hadn't played that trick on Mr. Holmes, Mrs. Mason wouldn't have gotten inside his room."

Ellie hung her head. "I know and I'm sorry."

"Well, you should be," said Terryl, surprised that Ellie really did seem to be sorry.

"You're always doing mean things," said Pam.

Ellie's head shot up. "I am not!"

"You locked me in the practice room yesterday."

"I know."

"That was bad," said Terryl.

Ellie's eyes filled with tears. "I guess I didn't know I was bad. I'm sorry. Honest I am. Please, forgive me."

Pam sighed. "We already did."

"You did?" asked Ellie in surprise.

Terryl nodded and Pam said, "We did because Jesus wanted us to. We love Jesus and we want to be like him."

Just then Mr. Holmes's door burst open and Mrs. Mason rushed out. Ellie caught the door before it banged shut. Terryl and Pam ran after Mrs. Mason and grabbed at her arms.

She glared at them. "Leave me alone! That old man is crazy!"

"What did you do to him?" asked Pam.

Ignoring the question, Mrs. Mason pushed open the door and stepped outside. Hot air rushed in and was shut off as the door closed. Mrs. Mason marched away from the tall building and out of sight.

"Let's see about Mr. Holmes," said Pam.

A few minutes later the twins stood in the doorway and saw Ellie beside Mr. Holmes. He sat in his rocker with his head down and his breathing ragged.

"Are you sure you're all right?" asked Ellie.

"Quite sure," he said in a weak voice.

"I could get you something."

He frowned at her. "How did you get in here?"

Terryl and Pam ran to his side. "We came to help you," said Terryl. "What can we do?"

He smiled and touched Terryl's shoulder as she

knelt beside him. "I will be just fine in a moment."

"Did Mrs. Mason hurt you?" asked Pam.

"No. She just screamed a lot and said that I couldn't keep her from the children. She said she'd call the police, and I told her to go ahead and call them." Mr. Holmes sat up and smiled shakily. "I wouldn't give an inch. She really expected me to give up my grandchildren, but I wouldn't—not after all these years of being without them. Finally she stormed out of here."

"Are you sure you're all right?" asked Terryl, peering closely at him.

"I'm fine. I need to relax just a moment more, and then I want to talk to my grandchildren. Dennis called and said he was coming. He should've been here. You girls go see if he got lost or something."

Ellie flushed and moved uneasily.

"Dennis didn't call you," said Pam, eyeing Ellie.

"It was me," said Ellie. In a rush of words she told Mr. Holmes what she'd done and why. She knelt before him and clasped her hands together. "I'm so sorry. I didn't think my phone call would make trouble for you."

Mr. Holmes looked into her eyes for a long moment, then he leaned forward and kissed her pink cheek. "I forgive you."

Ellie gasped and touched her cheek. Tears sparkled in her eyes.

"From now on think before you pull a prank on someone," said Mr. Holmes. "Think of the consequences to the other person."

"I will. I promise." Ellie slowly stood, her fingers still on her cheek where Mr. Holmes had kissed her. "I didn't know I would hurt anyone."

The doorbell rang and the girls jumped.

"Maybe it's Dad," said Terryl.

"Ask who it is before you open it," said Mr. Holmes. "I don't want Mrs. Mason in here again."

Terryl looked through the peephole but couldn't see anyone. "Who is it?" she asked uncertainly.

There was no answer and she asked louder, "Who is it?"

A strange voice said, "Open the door. I came for my children."

Terryl turned with a gasp and faced Mr. Holmes. "I think it's your daughter!"

Mr. Holmes pushed himself up and faced the door with his shoulders back and his head up. Tears filled his eyes. "Open the door for her, please."

Terryl's hand shook as she turned the knob, wondering what would happen next.

fOURTEEN
Tearful Reunion

Terryl slowly opened the door, her heart pounding. She could hear the soft intake of Pam's breath and Ellie's quick whisper to Pam.

Mr. Holmes stopped a few feet from the door and leaned heavily on his cane.

Pam rubbed her hands down her shorts and watched the woman who walked into the room. She was pretty and looked a few years older than Pam's mom. She wore the same kind of perfume that Beth did.

Ellie twisted her hair around her finger and for once didn't say anything.

Terryl felt the tension as Joy Hysell walked toward her father. Joy was short and slight with blonde hair and sad blue eyes. She wore a pink dress and sandals.

"Hello, Papa," Joy said stiffly.

"Joy. It's been a long time." He took a step toward her, but stopped at the look on her face.

"I came for my children." Joy glanced around. "Where are they? I'm going to take them home now." She turned back to Mr. Holmes, her eyes flashing. "What have you done with them?"

"They're safe. I want to talk to you before you see them."

Joy gripped her white purse tighter. "We have nothing to say."

Terryl suddenly realized the door was open. When she turned to close it she saw her dad standing there, and she sagged in relief. Just having him close made her feel better.

He came in, then closed the door and stood with his back against it, his arms crossed. "Garold, do you need a referee for this fight?" Richard asked in a light, teasing voice.

Joy spun around. "We don't need an audience *or* a referee!"

"Joy," Mr. Holmes said, "this is my friend Richard Tyler, his twins, and their friend Ellie. Richard, you are welcome to stay."

Mr. Holmes walked slowly back to his chair and sank down, then spoke to his daughter. "The children are in Richard's apartment and will remain there while we talk."

Joy took another step toward Mr. Holmes. "We have nothing to say! I want to take my children home now."

"Not yet, Joy."

"This is impossible!" cried Joy, flinging out one arm, then letting it drop back to her side.

"Please, talk to your father," said Terryl.

"Don't do anything to make his heart stop working," said Pam. Joy looked at Pam, startled, then turned to look at Mr. Holmes.

"Your heart, Papa?" she asked, a curious tone in her voice.

He waved a hand. "I just have to be careful."

"He had to have surgery," said Richard.

Joy frowned at Richard and the twins before she turned back to Mr. Holmes. "I don't want to do anything to harm you, but I *am* taking my children home now."

"They are beautiful children, Joy," said Mr. Holmes softly. "Gina looks like you did as a child."

Joy cleared her throat. "Yes, well, they are nice-looking children."

"Do you know I still keep pickles in the refrigerator just for you?"

"Don't—" Joy said, then she moistened her pink lips with the tip of her tongue. "Please don't."

"I was glad Rob sent me announcements of their birth. I wish that I could've been with you then. Your mother wanted to be there."

"Papa, don't," Joy insisted, pain in her voice. She nervously fingered the beads around her slender neck. "You should have let Mrs. Mason take the children with her."

"No!" Mr. Holmes's voice boomed out, and the twins jumped. Joy stood very still and watched her father. "Mrs. Mason wasn't a good baby-sitter for them. She hurt them and frightened them— that's why they came looking for me."

Joy frowned. "I thought she cared for the children. She seemed to be good with them. What do you mean she hurt them?"

"You ask Gina—and Billy."

"She is mean," said Ellie. "She pushed me and yelled at me."

Mr. Holmes got up from his chair and slowly crossed the room to his daughter. She stood very still, her eyes wide. "Joy," he said, "sit down and talk to me. Please."

"I can't."

"Why not?"

She helplessly shook her head. "It's been too long."

"It's time to forget and forgive." Mr. Holmes reached out and gently touched her cheek. "I should have tried to find you, to tell you that I loved you—but I couldn't do it. I was angry and hurt. And then I was afraid that if I did find you, you would walk away from me—just the way you are doing now."

"Oh, Papa."

"I love you, Joy. I've prayed for you every day. I want you back in my life. I want your children and your husband to be my family."

"No, you don't. It'll be the same."

Terryl bit her lip and waited. Pam pushed her hair behind her ears with an unsteady hand.

Mr. Holmes shook his head. "It can't be the same. You're older and I'm wiser. I can't dictate to you now. I know you're old enough to make your own choices."

Joy sniffed and rubbed her nose with the back of her hand. "I was sorry I left, but I was too stubborn to return home."

"You're here now," he whispered. "I love you and I want you to love me."

"Oh, Papa, of course I love you." She took a

hesitant step into his open arms, then clung to him and sobbed against his shoulder.

"A happy family," said Terryl.

Pam nodded and stepped closer to Terryl and Richard.

The doorbell rang and the twins jumped.

"Mrs. Mason!" cried Ellie, her eyes wide with fear. "Don't blame me this time."

"I doubt that it's Mrs. Mason," said Richard as he opened the door. Beth stood there with the children behind her.

"We couldn't wait any longer," Beth said with a small smile.

"You're just in time," said Richard, holding the door wider.

"Mom!" cried Dennis when he saw her.

"Mommy, Mommy!" Gina cried and ran to her mother.

Billy looked from his grandfather to his mother. "Are you still mad at him, Mom?"

"No, I'm not," Joy said, smiling at her father.

"Can he be our grandfather for real?" asked Gina.

"Yes," said Joy.

Gina took his hand and squeezed it.

Mr. Holmes motioned to Beth. "Beth, come meet my Joy. You saw her picture and shared our sorrow when she left. Now I want you to share our happiness. Joy, this is a very special friend of mine, Beth Harris. She helped your mother and me survive while you were away."

With a bright smile Beth held out her hand to

125

Joy. "I'm glad to meet you at last, Joy."

"Thank you for being there for my parents," said Joy.

Richard clamped his hand on Mr. Holmes's shoulder. "Garold, I'm taking my troop out of here. I'll talk to you later. You need time alone with your family."

"Thank you, Richard. And girls, thank you for all of your help."

After a few minutes of good-byes, Richard opened the door and waited for the twins. Ellie, Beth, and Timmy followed. In silence they all walked to the elevator.

"Why is everybody so quiet?" asked Timmy. "Are we sad?"

Beth laughed along with the others. "We're not sad at all, Timmy. We're happy, very happy."

Richard lifted Timmy high in his arms and smiled. "See this mouth, Timmy? Does that look like a sad mouth to you?"

Timmy giggled and hugged Richard's neck.

Ellie beckoned Terryl and Pam to her side and whispered, "I need to talk to you girls."

Terryl nodded and Pam looked suspicious.

"Dad, can we get off at Ellie's?" asked Terryl.

He nodded and they rode in silence to the ninth floor.

A few minutes later the twins faced Ellie in her bedroom. Her parents were talking in the living room and her brother was still at his friend's.

"Well?" asked Pam.

Ellie twisted her toe in the carpet. "I said I was

sorry for locking you in the practice room, Pam, but I wasn't really."

"We know," the twins said together.

Ellie blinked in surprise. "How could you know?"

"We could tell," said Terryl.

"But you forgave me."

Pam nodded. "Jesus wants us to forgive."

Ellie bit her lower lip. "He does?"

Pam nodded. "We want to do what Jesus wants, and so we forgave you even when you weren't sorry."

Ellie locked her fingers together. "I really am sorry now. Honest, I am. I know it was a bad thing for me to do. I know I've done lots of bad things."

"You're right about that," said Terryl.

"I didn't think about hurting others when I did bad things. I just did them." Ellie licked her lips. "Now I know and—I want to be good."

"I'm glad," said Terryl.

Pam looked right into Ellie's eyes. "You mean it this time, don't you?"

Ellie nodded. She cleared her throat and blinked tears from her eyes. "I just don't know if I can do it."

"You can," said Terryl.

"We ask Jesus to help us," said Pam. "And he does."

Ellie walked across the room, then turned and faced the twins. "Do you think Jesus . . . would help me like he helps you girls?"

"Of course!" cried Pam.

"Will you tell me how?" whispered Ellie.

"We'll tell you how," said Terryl.

"Let's sit down," said Ellie. She sank to the foot of her bed and picked up a pillow to hug. "I want to hear it all."

The twins scrambled to the middle of the bed and sat cross-legged, facing Ellie. They began to tell her the story of Jesus—how God sent his Son, Jesus, from heaven to die for all the bad things she ever did. Terryl told Ellie all she needed to do was to ask Jesus to forgive her and be her Savior. Then she would be a part of the most wonderful family in the world—God's family.

As Ellie bowed her head and prayed, Pam and Terryl smiled at each other. Mr. Holmes wasn't the only one to find a new family that day!